Heartland™
A Season of Hope

The hesitated at the top of the ramp, waiting for their eyesight to adjust to the gloom. Amy wiped her sticky hands on her jeans. One of the horses let out a loud, frightened snort, and when she peered in the direction of the sound, she made out two glinting eyes staring in her direction. "I'm going in," she said

"I'm right beside you," Ty said grimly.

Amy started to inch over the wooden floor towards the horse. "Steady there," she murmured.

The horse let out another snort and stepped backwards. Amy's eyes were getting used to the light by now, and she could make out the inside of the truck more clearly.

"Oh," she whispered. Her throat tightened, and she felt a rush of nausea as the smell of ammonia ached through her nose and mouth. Swallowing hard, Amy swept her gaze over the horses huddled miserably together. "How could anyone do this?"

Read all the books about Heartland:

Coming Home
After the Storm
Breaking Free
Taking Chances
Come What May
One Day You'll Know
Out of the Darkness
Thicker Than Water
Every New Day
Tomorrow's Promise
True Enough
Sooner or Later
Darkest Hour
Everything Changes
Love Is a Gift
Holding Fast

And look out for...

New Beginnings

Heartland™

A Season of Hope

Lauren Brooke

SCHOLASTIC

With special thanks to

Scholastic Children's Books,
Commonwealth House, 1–19 New Oxford Street,
London WC1A 1NU, UK
a division of Scholastic Ltd

London ~ New York ~ Toronto ~ Sydney ~ Auckland
Mexico City ~ New Delhi ~ Hong Kong

First published in the UK by Scholastic Ltd, 2004
Series created by Working Partners Ltd

Copyright © Working Partners Ltd, 2004

Heartland is a trademark of Working Partners Ltd

ISBN 0 439 96399 0

Printed and bound by Nørhaven Paperback A/S, Denmark

2 4 6 8 10 9 7 5 3

Chapter One

"If you guys don't hurry, we're going to miss the whole thing!" Lou teased as she looked at the state of the family room. The television set was facing the wall, temporarily pushed out of the way to make room for additional seating.

"That's not funny, Lou." Amy shot her sister a playful scowl as she gave the sofa one final heave. "Phew!" she panted. "That should do it. Now we just have to turn the TV around."

"Thank goodness! My back couldn't have taken much more." Ty collapsed in a chair and surveyed their handiwork with a laugh. "I don't think any of you have a future in interior design."

Amy rolled her eyes at Joni, who was at the opposite end of the sofa, but she had to admit her boyfriend had a point. There were two sofas and an oversize chair all crowded in front of the old television. It was congested, but Amy knew everyone would want a good view of the TV.

Lou returned to the room balancing a tray full of chips, cookies and sodas. "I hate to interrupt, but is there any way one of you could put this on the coffee table? I can't get through."

"Sorry, Lou," Amy said, reaching over Grandpa's recliner to grasp the tray by its handles.

It seemed everything was in place for the Heartland crew

to watch the long-awaited news feature together. Over the past several weeks a local news team had been following Heartland's progress with Venture, a police horse that had become famous not only for his heroic role in the rescue of some children during a tornado, but also for his resulting injuries. Venture's lack of response to treatment had generated tremendous media buzz. Now that the horse was showing improvement, the final news report was scheduled to air that night as a special-interest story at the end of the local news.

Everyone had gathered for the event. In addition to the core Heartland crew, Joni, the newest stable hand, was there. Grandpa's girlfriend, Nancy, had made a special trip as well. And Scott, who was both Lou's fiancé and their preferred vet, was on hand to offer his expert opinion of the show.

Amy frowned as she looked at the set-up again. "Do you think the TV should come forward a little?"

"No!" Ty and Joni shouted in unison just as Jack and Scott walked in from the kitchen.

Jack looked bemused as he surveyed the jumbled state of the room. Normally, the two blue sofas were on either side of the fireplace, with the television set tucked away in the alcove. "Now I know why we don't watch much TV," Jack commented with a smile.

"Who knows?" Scott said as he sat down and helped himself to a soda. "If Heartland gets much more famous, you might have to leave the room like this all the time!"

Jack switched on the television set and joined Lou and

Nancy while Joni sat in the chair in between the sofas.

Amy felt hot from moving the furniture, so she quickly scooped up her hair and tied it up in a knot. She passed Ty and Joni a soda before sitting down. "I hope it was the right decision, letting them come in and film while we were working," she said as the theme music for the local news began. Her stomach churned with anticipation.

Ty squeezed her hand. "You've just got last-minute nerves," he said in a reassuring tone. "I'm sure it will be great."

Amy picked up the bowl of chips and offered them first to Ty and then to Joni, who shook her head. "I don't feel like eating, either," Amy confessed sympathetically.

Joni had become involved in Venture's recovery very soon after she took Ben's place as a stable hand at Heartland. In fact, it was her suggestion that they try acupuncture, which her mom used at their stable in Alberta, Canada. Acupuncture had given them their first breakthrough with the police horse.

Suddenly Lou exclaimed, "This is it!"

Amy's attention snapped back to the television set. Jack reached for the remote control to turn up the volume as Kate Rogers, the slim, dark-haired reporter who had become a familiar face around Heartland, smiled into the camera. She gave a brief rundown of Venture's story. She began by describing how his human partner had bravely rescued some children from a car junkyard and how, in the process, Venture had been badly injured when he was struck by falling tyres.

"Police vets treated Venture with conventional methods,"

3

Kate Rogers explained. "But nothing eased his pain and depression. It seemed the police horse was destined for an early retirement. That is, until his partner, Sergeant Mark García, sought out Venture's last hope – a special place known as Heartland."

Amy felt her cheeks turn red. "A little melodramatic, isn't it?" she muttered.

"Shh," Lou said as the scene on the television set cut from Kate Rogers to an outside shot of Heartland's stable block next to the white farmhouse. The yard looked immaculate and tidy, and hanging baskets of flowers added splashes of red and yellow.

"Wow," Jack commented. "It looks great."

Amy nodded, sharing his pride. It was odd watching everything that was so familiar to her on television, as if she were seeing it through someone else's eyes.

The picture cut to an image of Venture standing in the schooling ring. His coat gleamed like burnished bronze, and his eyes were bright and alert.

Kate Rogers' voice sounded over the picture. "At Heartland, horses are treated with a variety of alternative methods." The camera zoomed out to show Amy flicking a longline at Venture, who obediently moved to the outside of the ring. It was obvious that his joints were still stiff from his old injury and the enforced rest following it. His head wasn't fully arched and his stride was short, but he broke into a canter at Amy's command.

Kate Rogers continued with her commentary. "Sergeant García

was convinced that he would never ride Venture on patrol again, but thanks to Heartland's innovative techniques, they are about to be reunited." Amy smiled as the camera focused on Sergeant García. He looked a little awkward, and his gaze flickered sideways to the lens. But then his eyes softened as he watched Venture canter past.

At that point, Kate Rogers asked Ty to explain what was happening in the ring. Amy listened as Ty described the incredible healing bond that could be created through join-up.

Ty shifted his weight on the sofa. "Is that what I sound like?" he questioned.

"Everyone wonders that when they hear their voice being played back to them," Scott told him.

"You sound just fine to me." Amy gave him a quick smile before returning her attention back to the set.

As she watched the television screen and saw Venture regarding her at the centre of the ring, Amy felt a powerful surge of emotion. She had watched other people join up before, but seeing Venture take his first tentative step towards her was incredible.

"This is the moment when we know the horse has put his trust in us," Ty said softly.

Amy was suddenly reminded of how her mom had looked the last time she had watched her do a join-up. While each join-up was special, the fundamentals were always the same. Amy felt a stinging of tears, not just of sadness but also of gratitude for the huge gift her mother had left in the healing work at Heartland. She glanced across to meet Jack and Lou's gazes. In that moment they shared a special, silent acknowledgment of just how far they all had come since Marion's death.

The scene on the television changed again to show Amy standing next to Sergeant García on one side of Venture, with Joni and Ty on the other side.

"Amy, tell us a little more about the methods you used to accomplish Venture's astonishing recovery," Kate Rogers said in a warm tone.

Listening to herself, Amy was surprised at how confident she sounded. She remembered feeling flustered during the interview, but none of that came across as she began to describe Venture's treatment. "Venture didn't respond well to join-up at first. His reaction suggested that he was still in a lot of pain and so we had to rethink our approach."

Next, Amy explained how Joni had initially proposed acupuncture, which was a new method for Heartland. Kate Rogers then probed Joni about the history of the therapy and its success with Venture. Everyone had a chance to contribute before the reporter turned to Sergeant García to end her report.

"We're thrilled to have Venture back on the force," the sergeant said. "We've got a fitness programme planned, so he'll be back in shape for street work soon."

"That's terrific news," Kate Rogers replied enthusiastically. "And I'm sure that everyone here wishes you both all the best."

"Thanks," said Sergeant García, and he turned away from the camera to rub Venture's nose. "I never thought I'd get to work with him again," he admitted. There was a slight catch to his voice when he added, "I can't thank everyone at Heartland enough for what they've done for us."

Amy felt a lump in her throat as Kate Rogers paused for dramatic effect and then turned to face the camera. "Well, that's the end of our special report about this very brave horse, and I know I speak for everyone who's watching when I say how delighted we are that this is one story with a very happy ending."

Chapter Two

As soon as the programme returned to the day's headlines, everyone started talking at once.

"It was a great report." Lou reached across to give Amy a hug. "You guys sounded so impressive. Nice work!"

Amy hugged her sister back. In the kitchen, the phone began to ring. "I'll get it," Lou said, letting go of Amy.

"I bet it won't stop ringing all night after that," Nancy said, giving Jack a pat on the back.

Amy looked at her grandfather. "Venture looked really good, didn't he?"

"Sure did. It's certainly not done our reputation any harm," he said, leaning over and squeezing Amy's shoulder. "I'm very proud of the way you made sure everyone was included in the report," he whispered, his eyes intent on his granddaughter's face.

Amy reached up and placed her hand on his, feeling a bubble of contentment rise inside her chest. Jack stood up and began to collect the empty soda cans.

Amy turned to Joni. "It's all thanks to your mom, really, the way she was able to come down and do the acupuncture on Venture herself. The difference that she made is amazing."

Joni nodded enthusiastically. "She's a pretty amazing person," she agreed.

"You know, I'll be the first to admit I was shocked by the

results. After seeing that, I wouldn't mind taking a course myself," Scott said thoughtfully.

"I can give you my mom's number if you'd like to talk to her about it," Joni offered.

"That would be great, thanks," Scott said. "Well, I'd better go and see if Jack needs a hand with the dishes. I can't have Lou thinking that I'm lazy, or she might not marry me."

"What, so you're just going to let her find out afterwards, you mean?" Amy joked, ducking as Scott threw a cushion at her.

Ty caught the cushion mid-air before it reached Amy. He then tossed it back on to the sofa and slipped his hand into Amy's to give it a quick squeeze. "The interview was terrific. I can't get over how great Venture looked on camera. And Joni," he said, looking in the new stable hand's direction, "you came across really well, like an old Heartland pro."

"Thanks, Ty." Joni couldn't stop a delighted smile from spreading across her face.

Ty looked down at Amy. "And I guess you didn't do too badly, either," he teased.

"Well, thanks!" Amy laughed, holding her hands out for him to pull her up. "I'll try not to let it go to my head." She bent down to retrieve the bowl of chips that had been left on the floor. "Can you stay for dinner, Joni?"

Joni shook her head. "No, thanks. Ben said he'd come by early to pick me up."

Amy smiled. "Well, I wish you could, but I know you're pretty dependent on Ben for rides just now," she said. "But I think you'd be doing Ty a favour if you stayed. Now he'll have to listen to us rave about the interview all by himself. He won't be able to shut us up!" She glanced across at Ty and felt some of her excitement fade as he shook his head.

"Sorry, but I can't stay, either. I promised to eat at home tonight," Ty explained. "Mom's cooking dinner before Dad leaves for Pennsylvania. It's a big trip for him. After his company got taken over by new management, several people got laid off, and he feels really lucky that he still has his job."

Amy felt a stab of frustration. That afternoon she had baked a lemon cheesecake from one of Lou's recipes. Amy had been quite proud of her culinary effort and had planned to surprise Ty – cheesecake was one of his favourites. She tried not to let disappointment creep into her voice as she said, "That's OK." But judging by the way Ty frowned slightly, it was clear that she hadn't succeeded. Amy forced a smile on to her face. "I probably won't get a word in edgeways between Lou, Grandpa and Scott, anyway."

She followed Ty out to his car, still inwardly struggling with the fact that the evening would not be what she had planned. Before getting in, he turned to face her. "I'm really sorry, Amy. You know I'd love to stay, but I promised my mom I'd get home. It's important to her that we're all together as a family tonight before Dad leaves tomorrow." He hesitated. "Besides, things have been different with Dad since my accident. It's been better." His green eyes looked thoughtful.

Amy frowned. She wanted Ty to do the right thing for his mom. They had a good relationship, but Ty's dad was a different story. He had never endorsed Ty's decision to work at Heartland, and Amy thought that Ty's accident had only complicated matters. Amy knew they were attempting to make things work, yet she suspected most of the effort was on Ty's part. Just as she was about to ask Ty to explain how things had improved, he reached out and wrapped his arms around her. As she rested her head against his shoulder, Amy couldn't help wondering how Ty handled his dad's constant nagging about his job. She knew how much she relied on Grandpa and Lou for support.

"It's OK. I understand," she said, hoping that Ty wouldn't be let down again.

"I knew you would." Ty smiled before bending down to kiss her.

They were interrupted by the beep of a horn and a car pulling up alongside them. Amy gave Ty a shy smile as they waited for Ben to park his car.

"Hi!" Amy stepped forward to open the driver's door as Ben pushed his sunglasses back over his blond hair and greeted her with a huge grin.

"Guess who's just been offered a position at Nick Halliwell's stable?"

"Really? That's great!" Amy exclaimed, giving him a hug. Ben had left Heartland to pursue showjumping, and earning a place as one of Nick Halliwell's working pupils was a major step forward for his career.

"Congratulations," Ty called as he climbed into his truck. "That's great news." He stuck his hand out the window to give Ben a high five.

"Thanks," Ben said.

"I've got to go, but I'll catch up with you soon and you can tell me more about it," Ty said apologetically as he started up the engine. Ben and Amy stood back and waved as Ty left the yard.

"So, how did you manage to get a place at Nick Halliwell's?" Amy demanded, thinking of how competitive it was to work for someone with Nick's credentials. She became aware of footsteps behind her, and Joni joined them in time to overhear her question.

"No way! You've been offered a place at Nick Halliwell's?" Joni's voice rose in excitement. "The Nick Halliwell of international showjumping fame?"

Ben laughed. "I'm beginning to find your amazement a little insulting."

"It goes without saying that he's lucky to have you and Red, of course," Amy reassured him.

"That's better," Ben said. He leaned back against his car door and took a more serious tone. "Nick just called me today to say that one of his pupils gave notice because she's starting her own stables. He said Red and I were his first choice as replacements." Ben raised one eyebrow. "He also said that he hoped I would share some of what I learned in my time at Heartland with his other trainers."

Amy felt herself blush with pleasure. "He said that?"

"He sure did," said Ben. "I guess it was worthwhile getting to know you after all."

He threw a few lighthearted jabs at Amy's shoulder, and she

pretended to punch him back before breaking into fresh laughter. Ben's good mood was infectious.

"Sorry to bring up more mundane matters, but when do you start?" Joni put in. "I knew those free rides were too good to last."

Ben lowered his head and tried to look sympathetic. "I know." He sighed. "Believe me, knowing that I wouldn't be able to chauffeur you any more almost made me turn the job down, but Nick talked me into starting tomorrow."

"Well," Joni replied, "I guess it's time for me to get my own wheels, but I appreciated your services while they lasted." She turned to Amy. "Do you mind if I take my day off tomorrow so I can go and look at some cars?"

"Not at all. Why don't you give Ty a call and ask him to go with you?" Amy suggested. "Soraya's coming over, so she can help me in the yard."

"As long as you don't mind, that sounds great," Joni thanked her, the corners of her eyes wrinkling slightly as she smiled.

Ben glanced at his watch. "We should get going," he said. "I've got to go over to Nick's tonight to sign my contract." He opened the car door.

"Congrats again!" Amy called through the open window as she waved them both off.

Once the car had disappeared down the driveway, Amy headed to the feed room. She felt a glow of happiness as she thought over Ben's news. Although everyone at Heartland missed him, Amy had come to realize that he had made the best decision. Her thoughts were interrupted by an impatient whinny from inside the barn. Sundance clearly thought his supper was overdue! Amy smiled as she made a start on filling the evening haynets.

Ty arrived early the next morning to get some chores done before he went car shopping with Joni. He began leading the horses down to the fields as Amy filled water buckets. "Do you want me to leave Jasmine and Sundance for you and Soraya?" Ty called as he passed her.

"Yeah, that's great." Amy pushed a strand of hair out of her eyes. She felt a quick thrill of excitement at the thought of a long trail ride. She remembered she wanted to ask Ty about how the dinner with his parents had gone, but she decided to wait until later, when they would have more time to talk. "You should get going now," she said, stacking the last of the buckets. "I can finish up here."

"Thanks," Ty said. "You just have to collect all the haynets. Everything else is done."

Amy slipped from stall to stall, unclipping empty haynets. Sundance watched as she walked down the centre aisle and let out a low, expectant nicker. Amy stopped to stroke his velvety nose. "Yes, you're very clever. You know we're going out, don't you? I'll be back when Soraya gets here," she promised as he pushed impatiently at her hand.

When she returned to the house, Amy found that Soraya had already arrived. She and Lou were poring over some brochures spread on the kitchen table. Nancy was there, too, and was clearing away the breakfast plates to make more room.

"What's going on?" Amy asked.

"Hi." Soraya looked up and smiled. "I just got here, but I couldn't resist looking at these brochures before coming out."

"They're for wedding tents," Lou explained, pulling out a chair for Amy. "Nancy brought them over."

Amy gave Lou a good look in an attempt to gauge her sister's reaction to Nancy's involvement. Amy couldn't help but remember Lou's initial resentment of Nancy's unsolicited advice.

"Aren't they fabulous?" Lou went on excitedly, and Amy relaxed as she realized that Lou was fine with Nancy's help this time. The two had obviously come to an understanding, and now they both were devoted to planning a divine wedding.

"Oh, look at this one!" Soraya exclaimed, pushing a brochure towards them.

"That's one of my favourites," Nancy cooed.

Amy looked at the photo of a large white canvas tent strung with delicate white lights. Lou let out a breath, and Amy pictured her sister in a long ivory dress, standing alongside one of the interior pillars.

"It's beautiful. It would be perfect for the reception, Lou," she said enthusiastically. Then a thought struck her and she frowned. "But weren't you saying that tents are expensive?"

"Nancy's got connections." Her sister looked up and winked.

"A friend of my late husband's owns a tent company," Nancy explained, "and when I happened to mention that I knew someone who was getting married, he promised a discount. Of course," she glanced across at Lou, "you shouldn't feel that you have to choose one of his tents."

Lou smiled with real warmth in her eyes. "I love them. I think it's a wonderful idea," she said.

Nancy smiled in return and leaned over the table to look at the picture Lou was holding. She spoke quickly, her voice showing her excitement. "I can just picture this one out on the lawn, maybe with some ivy garlands woven around the poles. I'll give Jon a call later to confirm, but he said he could give a twenty per cent discount," she added.

"Really?" Lou opened her eyes wide. "That would mean we could afford the larger tent with room for a hundred guests!" She pushed her chair away from the table and stood up. "Scott and I were ready to settle for one that seated sixty. He'll be thrilled if we can invite forty more guests. He knows so many people!"

Amy had rarely heard Lou's voice ring with so much enthusiasm, and as she looked into her sister's sparkling cornflower-blue eyes, she felt a pang of relief. She was glad that the wedding plans seemed to be going so smoothly. Amy reached out to squeeze her sister's hand. It was great having such a happy occasion for them all to look forward to!

Chapter Three

Amy leaned forward to take her weight out of the saddle and patted Sundance's neck. "We're almost to the top, then we can have a good long canter," she told him.

Amy glanced over her shoulder at Soraya and Jasmine, who had fallen behind. She couldn't help smiling at the way the dainty black mare was picking her way over the rougher areas of the trail, unlike Sundance, who strode boldly forward despite the uneven terrain.

Amy halted Sundance at the top of the hill and, shielding her eyes from the glare of the sun, waited for her friend to join her. For early spring, it was turning out to be an incredibly hot day. Amy flapped her T-shirt to cool off as she took in the view. From high on Teak's Hill she could just make out the rooftops of the buildings at Heartland and the distant shapes of the grazing horses. The fields looked like a patchwork quilt, divided into squares by trees and hedges.

Amy loved Saturdays, when she had the satisfaction of knowing that all of the morning stable work was finished and, instead of having to head for school, she could tack up and head out on a long trail ride.

With a final scrabbling of hooves against loose stones, Jasmine and Soraya caught up. Soraya patted the black pony's damp neck. "Are you thinking what I'm thinking?" she asked.

Amy grinned. "What, that every day should be a Saturday?"

Soraya's face broke into a wide smile. "Absolutely! What would a Saturday be without a trail ride? And," she shortened her reins, her eyes bright with laughter, "what would a trail ride be without a canter?" Her voice carried behind her as Jasmine darted forward at the first nudge of Soraya's heels.

Laughing, Amy loosened her reins and let Sundance take off after them. "Go on, boy!" she shouted. The wind whipped her hair as Sundance's unhindered stride carried them easily ahead of the black mare. The trees lining the path turned into a blur as Amy urged Sundance to go faster, and the pony extended into a full gallop. When Amy finally squeezed the reins to slow down, she could sense his disappointment in the backwards flick of his ears. "I know, boy," Amy commiserated with the pony. "It's never fun to stop."

The ponies settled into a walk side by side, giving Amy and Soraya a chance to talk. Looking at her best friend, Amy realized how little time they'd spent together recently. With Lou's wedding plans, Joni settling in at Heartland, and their work with Venture, Amy had had even less time than usual. Her schedule was always busy, and now that Soraya had the additional commitments of the drama programme and dating Matt, the two friends rarely had the chance for a leisurely trail ride.

And, Amy admitted to herself, there was something else. Recently, things hadn't felt the same between them. Soraya seemed to always be stressing out about her relationship with Matt – and venting her suspicions to Amy.

"So," Amy asked, mentally crossing her fingers, "how are things now with you and Matt?"

Soraya hesitated before saying, "OK." She fiddled with a strand of Jasmine's mane, and Amy knew her best friend well enough to know that she was holding something back.

"Really?" Amy questioned.

Soraya glanced across, and Amy saw a troubled expression in her eyes. "I'm still not a hundred per cent happy," she admitted.

Amy couldn't help feeling a slight twinge of impatience. Matt was a great guy – she couldn't figure out why Soraya was determined to find problems in their relationship. "What's worrying you now?" she asked, trying to sound sympathetic.

Soraya bit her lower lip. "Well, you know how I feel about the fact that Matt is still friends with Ashley?"

Amy nodded. Soraya had been very upset when Matt had spent time working with Ashley Grant on a homework assignment without telling her. And it didn't help that Ashley had publicized their study session like it was a secret rendezvous, Amy added to herself. While Amy thought Soraya's doubts about Matt were unfounded, she knew Ashley would go out of her way to make things difficult for her friend – usually with blatant reminders that she had dated Matt herself.

"It's not that I don't trust Matt," Soraya continued, "but I'm sure Ashley wants him back. I mean, she still calls him on his cellphone."

"Well, if you know that, then it's obvious that Matt's not trying to hide anything from you," Amy pointed out. "If you ask me, Ashley is just trying to bother you, as usual. She must love knowing that she's making you jealous."

Soraya made a face. "Is it that obvious?"

"Oh, just a bit." Amy smiled.

They stopped at a gate leading into a field, and Amy leaned forward to open it. Soraya rode through with a thoughtful expression on her face.

"Hey! Earth to Soraya," Amy teased, shutting the gate behind them as Sundance made a neat turn on his haunches.

But Soraya didn't smile in return. Instead she said worriedly, "I just think that Matt shouldn't let Ashley call him so much. It's practically every day!"

Amy sighed inwardly. Sundance snatched at the reins and swished his tail, obviously anxious for another canter across the soft green grass stretching out in front of them. "We've both been friends with Matt for ages," she reminded Soraya. "If I had to put my trust in someone, Matt would be right up there."

Soraya nodded. "I know," she said. "I'm sorry I'm going on about it. It's just that if Matt and I split up, then I'll have lost more than a boyfriend. I'll have lost one of my best friends."

"That's not going to happen," Amy said. "You and Matt are great together, as long as you're not bashing him about Ashley, that is!"

Soraya suddenly grinned. "Ashley bashing – now I could go for that!"

As the two girls broke into laughter, Sundance sensed the change in their spirits and broke into a trot. Amy quickly brought him back under control before turning to Soraya. "I think Sundance wants to stretch his legs again!"

"Let's go!" Soraya called back, collecting Jasmine.

This is more like it, Amy thought, emptying her mind of all worries as they raced across the field. She was glad she'd talked things through with Soraya and even happier that the discussion was over. She gathered Sundance and pointed him at a small fence that brought them back on to the trail.

"Good girl!" Soraya called as Jasmine sailed over the fence alongside Sundance.

Amy grinned at her, and they cantered on together along the ridge, the view spread out for miles beneath them.

When they clattered into the yard, Amy was surprised to see Ty sweeping it. "You're back sooner than I expected!"

Ty nodded. "We found a great car – only the second one we looked at. Joni's ecstatic."

"That's great." Amy slipped down from Sundance and looped the reins over her arm. "Where is she?"

"In with Venture." Ty jerked his head towards the middle stable just as the door swung open and Joni appeared, brushing off her jeans.

"So, what's the car look like?" Soraya called to Ty as she ran Jasmine's stirrups up their leathers.

"Typical girl!" Ty teased. "Not interested in the engine size or fuel mileage; you only want to know what it looks like!"

"Very funny!" Soraya said, pretending to look indignant. "I was going to ask all that after you answered the most important question."

"Which is?" Ty raised his eyebrows.

"What colour is it?" Soraya and Amy spoke at the same time before bursting into laughter. Amy broke off as she noticed Joni standing with her eyebrows raised in mock disbelief.

"What's up?" she asked, looking from one to the other.

"Nothing," Ty said hurriedly.

"Really?" Joni folded her arms. "What Ty means," she said, turning to Amy and Soraya, "is that when we looked at the first car, he thought it was a great buy. Unfortunately, I pointed out a few details – like the fact that when I unscrewed the engine oil filler cap, there was a white film inside the cap, which suggests the head gasket might have blown. And when the engine was started, blue smoke came out of the exhaust, which is a sure-fire sign that the pistons are faulty."

"Oh, no!" Amy grinned, looking at Ty, who turned red. "Even I know faulty pistons aren't a good thing."

"Don't worry, Ty," Soraya joined in the teasing. "I'm sure you were able to advise Joni on which colour to go for!" All three girls broke into fresh laughter, and Ty shook his head in despair, trying to suppress a smile.

"Yes," he offered. "It's red."

Once Soraya had gone, Ty and Amy took Venture down to the schooling ring to fit in a session before lunch. As they halted the bay horse on the soft surface, he snorted and pawed at the sand.

"Look at that!" Amy exclaimed. "He's actually impatient to get started." Venture nodded his head up and down as if agreeing with her.

"Wait a second, boy." Amy laughed, patting his neck. "I need to get these knots out of the lunge line." She turned to Ty, her fingers still unravelling the ties. "How did things go with your dad last night?"

"OK, thanks," he replied. He reached out his hand to pull a piece of straw out of Venture's mane.

Amy waited for Ty to continue, and when he didn't she prompted, "I bet he's looking forward to his long trip."

Ty nodded. "It was kind of weird. I haven't seen him in such a good mood in a long time. He kept talking about how the people who are in charge of his company now have made all these changes. Mind you, I think he's relieved he still has a job. They only kept a handful of the original drivers." Ty rested his hand on Venture's neck and seemed to study it. "You know," he continued, "he even talked about how great it is that they're trusting him with this big new client in Pennsylvania. It'll be good if he can stop worrying about things."

Despite his optimistic words, there was a flat tone in Ty's voice, and Amy sensed he was holding back on her.

"What is it?" she asked softly, shifting so she could see Ty's face.

Ty hesitated and then admitted, "When he thought he was going to get laid off, Dad started pressuring me, saying I should find a job that pays more."

"I thought you said things had been better since your accident." Amy's voice was gruff with indignation.

"We are getting along better." Ty quickly rose to Brad's defence. "Last night he even said we should go bowling when he gets back."

"But we're not talking about bowling," Amy retorted. "We're talking about how he feels about you working at Heartland." She stroked Venture's neck as the bay horse shifted his weight, sensing their tension.

Ty shrugged. "Look, he only said that thing about another job once, and he hasn't brought it up again since he got this contract," Ty shared. "I mean, in his eyes, the accident was a sign that I should give up working around horses and find something else to do."

When Ty said that, Amy suddenly remembered overhearing Mr Baldwin in Ty's hospital room. She recalled that his voice had been much softer when speaking to his unconscious son. He had more or less said he thought Ty would be smart to forget about all the "horse business" and be more practical. Amy wasn't surprised that Brad Baldwin held Heartland somewhat responsible. Amy herself had felt that guilt, knowing that she and Ty had entered the barn together the night of the storm, but she was the only one who made it out safely. But now Ty was better and he still wanted to be there.

She couldn't understand why Ty's opinion meant so little to his father. She bit back her angry words, realizing that Ty was already under enough pressure from his dad without getting more from her. But even so, she couldn't hide the edge to her voice by changing the subject. "Should we work Venture over some trotting poles today?"

"That's a good idea," said Ty, sounding relieved. "I'll go set up the poles while you warm him up." Before he went, he unbuttoned the shirt that he was wearing over a blue T-shirt. "Is it me, or is it hot today?" he asked as he tied his shirt around his waist.

"It's more like summer than spring," Amy agreed, reaching

up to unbuckle Venture's halter. Venture knew the routine by now, and the moment he felt that he was free, he snorted and trotted to the far end of the ring. Amy smiled and felt some of her tension disappear as the big bay automatically broke into a canter when he reached the corner of the schooling ring. He was still not lengthening his stride as much as she would have liked, but she knew that exercising him over the trotting poles would really help to stretch his muscles.

Amy flicked out her lunge line to drive Venture harder than she had before and was pleased when he didn't seem at all stressed by working more strenuously. His neck was arched, and he held his black tail high so it streamed behind him in the air like a banner. It was clear that he was enjoying himself. When Venture dropped his head and looked as if he were chewing the air, Amy sent him around the ring a few times more before turning away from him and lowering the lunge line. At once Venture slowed, recognizing the invitation to join her. For the first time since she had been doing join-up with the police horse, he actually pushed Amy's back with his nose when he walked up behind her and lipped her shoulder. Amy laughed out loud and turned to rub Venture's forehead. As Venture's confidence grew, he was beginning to reveal a spunky personality that must have made him a wonderful partner for Sergeant García.

Amy walked Venture down to the bottom end of the ring where Ty had finished laying out the trotting poles in an arc. He quickly paced out the distance between the poles again to check that they were correct for Venture's stride. When he reached the last pole he gave Amy a thumbs-up.

To begin, Amy led Venture over the poles at a quiet walk. The horse pricked his ears and stepped over them carefully, snorting when he knocked a pole with his back hoof. Amy patted his neck and urged him into a trot for the second circuit before finally unclipping the rein and sending him around on his own. Venture held his tail high, his eyes calm as he stepped freely over the poles.

"He's had a hard road to recovery, but it looks like he's going to be fine," Ty remarked.

"It sure does," Amy replied happily, watching Venture give a half buck as if he shared their sense of achievement.

Amy and Ty continued to work Venture over the trotting poles in the afternoons after school. By the end of the week, his stride was longer and more fluid, and Amy felt a sense of satisfaction as she watched him trot and then canter easily over the poles in their last session on Friday evening. Out of the corner of her eye she saw Mark García standing at the fence alongside Ty. He had arranged to pick up Venture and take him back to the police stables that day.

Mark waved. "He's looking almost like his old self," he called through cupped hands. Amy waved back and returned her attention to Venture, who was stepping over the final pole of the arc. She lowered the lunge line, and the big bay approached her and blew into her hair. Amy pressed her cheek against his velvety nose. She was suddenly certain he understood that she and the others had helped him through his dark and painful journey, that he had a sense of how far he had come.

"It's time for you to go home," she whispered, realizing how much she was going to miss the big horse.

Amy handed Venture over to Sergeant García at the entrance to the arena and smiled as he pulled at the bay's ears and patted his neck. Venture pushed at Mark playfully before walking beside him up to the yard, where a trailer was waiting.

"It's so great to be taking him home," Sergeant García told Amy and Ty as he unbuckled Heartland's halter and slipped on one of his own. Amy took their halter from him and gave Venture's nose a final stroke.

"Be good, boy." Ty held out a mint, which Venture lipped off his hand and crunched loudly.

Joni appeared from the tack room with a box of travelling equipment. "I'll give you a hand putting his wraps on," she told Sergeant García in an unusually flat tone. Looking at the new stable hand's rigid expression, Amy guessed that Joni was feeling exactly how she and Ty used to when they had to say goodbye to a horse that they had devoted themselves to treating.

After bolting the ramp with Venture safely inside the trailer, Sergeant García shook their hands in turn. "There was a time when I thought he would never pull through," he said. "I can't really put into words what this means to me."

"We're just thrilled to know that you two are a team again," Amy said.

Sergeant García nodded. "It would have been a terrible waste if we'd had to retire him. He's one of the best." He looked at Joni. "Your idea of acupuncture certainly did the trick. We owe you a lot."

Joni's cheeks turned red. "Don't mention it," she said. "I'm glad to have helped such a special horse."

"Be safe," Ty said as Sergeant García walked to the cab and climbed up alongside the driver.

"You, too," Mark García called over the sound of the engine starting up. They all waved as the trailer slowly pulled away.

"I'm really going to miss Venture," Joni said with a sigh.

Amy gave her arm a squeeze. "We all are. I just try to remember that seeing a horse leave means we've done our job. But sometimes a special horse comes along and makes it harder than usual to say goodbye."

Joni looked at the disappearing trailer, her blue eyes serious. "I know what you mean. Believe me."

Amy suddenly became aware of the telephone ringing from inside the house. "I'd better go and answer it. I don't think Lou's around," she told them, and quickly headed indoors.

"I was just about to hang up," said a familiar voice when Amy picked up.

"Ben! Sorry it rang so long. I don't know where Lou is. What's going on?"

"Everything's great, thanks." Ben sounded very upbeat. "Red and I are both settling in, but Nick says we've got an uphill battle if we want to knock Daniel and Storm off the number-one spot!"

"I'm sure you'll have fun trying," Amy said, knowing Ben's competitive nature. She crossed to the chair in the corner of the room and cradled the phone on her shoulder as she began pulling off her boots. "I'm glad you're fitting in."

"Thanks. I'm even being sought as a consultant," Ben told her.

Amy couldn't tell if he was joking or not. "Really?" she said.

"There's a horse called Apollo on the yard," Ben offered in a more serious tone. "He's great, with an amazing jump. You'd love him!"

Amy frowned, uncertain where Ben was going.

"Anyway, Tara – Apollo's owner – is having trouble with him outside the schooling ring. I mean, he's a real Jekyll-and-Hyde character, in horse terms, at least. When he's doing flat work and jumping he's full of enthusiasm, but the moment she tries to take him out of the ring he's like a different horse."

"What does he do?" Amy asked, feeling a spark of interest.

"What doesn't he do? He pulls, spins around, refuses to go forward. He's fine in the barn and in the ring, but if she tries to veer him off the path between the two, he bolts back."

"That's bad news," Amy agreed, curling her legs up on the chair as she took in the information.

"Well, Tara's frustrated beyond belief. Nick's not too worried, since Apollo performs so well in the ring, but she wants to take him on the trails. Her last barn was strict and didn't let the horses on trails, so she had really been looking forward to checking out the woods behind Nick's place. It was one of her reasons for coming here." Ben paused. "Amy, I hope you don't mind, but I told her I'd mention it to you and see what you would suggest."

"That's fine," Amy said, trying not to show how delighted she was that Ben still valued her opinion, even though he was now at a top stable. "I think it would be best if I could come over and look at him. I'll see if I can work it in tomorrow."

"That would be great. I'll tell Tara." Ben sounded pleased. "She'll be thrilled – I've told her all about you."

"I'll try to get over after the morning feeds," Amy promised before saying goodbye. She hung up the phone and gave a quick clap of joy. She couldn't wait to go to Nick's yard, especially since it meant that she would be able to see Daniel and Storm, too.

She was suddenly aware that Scott and Lou were standing in the doorway watching her. "Is everything all right?" Lou asked, looking amused.

"Yes." Amy grinned a little self-consciously, dropping her hands from their celebratory applause. "Venture's gone home, so that's one more success story for us."

"That's good news," Lou smiled, looking at Scott.

Amy sensed that she didn't have Lou's full attention. "Venture leaving means that we have a space to fill," she pointed out. "We can contact whoever is next on the waiting list."

Lou nodded absently. "I guess so. Who was that on the phone?"

"It was Ben," she said tightly, feeling like Lou wasn't going to be interested in her answer anyway. "He wants me to go over to Nick's yard tomorrow to see if I can help with one of their horses."

"I can take you if you want," Scott offered, sitting down at the table. "I'd already planned to stop by there tomorrow to drop off some medication."

Amy glanced at Lou, whose eyes were sparkling. In fact, Amy realized they both looked pretty pleased with themselves. "What's going on?" she asked. "Where've you been?"

Lou smiled widely. "We've just dropped off some mail," she said. "More specifically, we've just sent off a cheque for the deposit on the tent." She crossed the room to Amy, who was fighting some familiar conflicting feelings. "I finally feel as if the wedding's really going to happen!" she declared, her voice brimming with happiness. But Lou didn't seem to notice that Amy was struggling to echo her excitement.

Chapter Four

Amy pulled a comb through her light brown hair before quickly tying it back in a ponytail. Scott's horn sounded outside as she raced out of her bedroom and down the stairs.

"Ready?" Winding down his window, the vet smiled at her.

"Sure am." Amy smiled back and slid on to the front passenger seat. As they began to pull out of the yard, another car pulled into the long driveway. "It's Soraya!" Amy exclaimed in surprise. "I thought she was going to watch Matt play basketball today."

"That's what Matt told me, too." Scott frowned. He stopped the Jeep and Amy jumped out.

"Thanks for the lift," Soraya called, waving to her mom before turning to face Amy.

"Hey, what's up? Are you OK?" Amy asked, noticing that Soraya's eyes were red.

"Not exactly," Soraya told her grimly.

Amy felt concern flood through her. "What's happened?"

"Matt and I went to the movies last night, and who should we bump into but Ashley. Bit of a coincidence, don't you think?" Without giving Amy a chance to reply, Soraya continued angrily, "She told Matt she was going to the match today to cheer him on! Can you believe it?"

Amy felt confused. She had thought that something really bad must have happened.

"So there's no way I'm going to cheer alongside Ashley. She can have Matt to herself," Soraya finished, looking as if she was torn between hitting something and bursting into tears.

"I'm sure that's not what he wants," Amy said with a frown. "Just because Ashley keeps after him doesn't mean Matt's interested."

"Want to bet?" Soraya snapped.

Amy felt taken aback and was relieved when Joni paused from pushing the wheelbarrow and called across the yard, "You off now?"

Amy nodded. "We shouldn't be too long."

"Take your time. I'm going to pick up my car this afternoon, but I'll make sure everything's done before I go. I want to hear about Apollo tomorrow!"

"Sure thing," Amy agreed.

Joni picked up the handles again. "Have a good time."

Soraya smiled and waved as Joni went off, whistling under her breath. She looked past Amy to the Jeep. "Where are you two going?"

Amy quickly told her about the conversation with Ben about Apollo. "I'd better go," she said apologetically. "I'm holding Scott up."

"Well, would you mind if I came along with you?" Soraya asked. "It's been a while since I saw Ben."

"Sure," Amy responded, but as they walked across to the Jeep she couldn't help wondering why Soraya was suddenly so intent on seeing Ben. Although Soraya had been interested in Ben once, it had been a long time ago, and they'd never been more than friends. By the time Ben had realized he liked her, Soraya and Matt were already an item. Amy sighed as she pulled open the passenger door. She was beginning to feel fed up with the Soraya and Matt saga, and was relieved that Scott was driving them to Nick Halliwell's yard. Soraya wouldn't say anything else about Matt with his older brother in the Jeep with them.

Amy was glad Scott had the air conditioner on. The spell of spring heat had not let up, and Amy was frustrated by the early, unrelenting temperatures. During the drive they discussed possible causes for Apollo's strange behaviour.

"Could he have had a bad experience when he was being ridden away from home one time?" Soraya suggested.

"That's would be the most obvious answer," Scott said. "What do you think, Amy?"

"It makes sense," Amy said slowly. "But Nick Halliwell is excellent with horses, and I'm sure he would have thought of that. It seems to be a mystery to everyone – including Apollo's owner."

"Well, whatever it is, it gives you a great reason for visiting Daniel and Storm," Soraya commented. "I bet you can't wait to see them again."

"I am looking forward to it," Amy admitted. "Although it's been a while since I've seen Storm. He might not even recognize me."

"You two had a strong bond. I'm sure he hasn't forgotten you," Soraya said loyally. Amy turned around in the seat to smile at her friend, but Soraya was staring absentmindedly out the window.

* * *

When they pulled into Nick Halliwell's yard, their attention was immediately taken by a beautiful dapple grey horse sailing over a course of jumps in the schooling ring. Ben was leaning on the fence, watching. Amy and Soraya made their way down a grassy bank to the ring while Scott went to find Nick.

Ben turned and gave them a warm smile of welcome. "Pretty good, aren't they?" he said, nodding his head towards the horse and rider who were gliding over an oxer.

"Very," Amy agreed as the grey cantered steadily on to the parallel bars. She watched the gelding clear them easily before she said, regretfully, "I'd love to stay and watch, but I know that Scott doesn't have a lot of time. Is Tara around, and Apollo?"

Ben grinned. "You're looking at them."

"Wow," Soraya said, leaning her arms on the fence alongside him.

Amy looked again at the horse and rider who had completed the course and were now cantering around the ring at a perfect, collected pace. "You weren't kidding when you said that Apollo behaved well in the ring," she commented.

At that moment Tara rode up to them. "Tara, this is my friend Amy, whom I told you about, and this is Soraya," Ben introduced them to the pretty redhead. A few curly strands of hair had escaped her braid and were blowing against her cheeks.

"Thanks so much for coming, Amy. Ben's told me a lot about you." Tara exchanged a warm smile with Ben, and Amy immediately sensed a spark between them.

She patted Apollo's damp neck and wondered if Soraya had

35

noticed, too, as her friend interrupted, "So, Ben, are you missing us all from Heartland?"

Ben gave an easy laugh. "Of course. If I could have stayed at Heartland and been focused on showing, I would have, but there was just no way. I think this was a good move for me." He shrugged and then gave Tara a quick glance.

Amy felt uncomfortable in the sudden silence and quickly suggested that Tara try riding Apollo out of the ring so they could see how he reacted. Tara paused to let down her stirrups from their jumping length and then turned Apollo around. At first the big grey gelding trotted alongside the fence eagerly, but when they reached the gate, he checked. Tara drove him strongly forward with her seat and legs until Apollo grudgingly walked out of the ring, his haunches taut beneath him. His body had lost its beautiful outline and his head came up, making his neck stiff and his back hollowed.

Ben ran ahead to open the gate that led into the fields, but the moment Tara tried to ride through, Apollo stopped dead. Once again, Tara anticipated his reluctance. But this time when she closed her heels on his sides, Apollo clamped down his tail and scooted backwards.

Amy watched Apollo's flattened ears and wide staring eyes. "He's not being naughty," she murmured. "He's scared."

After a few moments' struggle, Tara managed to ride Apollo through the gate, but clearly against the gelding's will. Snatching the reins from Tara's hands, he put his head down and gave a buck. It was obviously meant as a warning to his rider. Amy could see that if Tara kept pushing, he would give a bigger buck – this time in an attempt to unseat her. Amy noticed a heavy lather building on Apollo's neck, but this sweat was less from the heat than the agitation. Just as she was about to call out to Tara to bring him back towards the stable, Apollo wheeled around and bolted towards them.

Ben made a grab for him, but Apollo swerved. Amy watched anxiously as Tara gathered the reins and managed to turn Apollo in a circle. She kept him cantering on the grass beside the training ring, her face set, steadily decreasing the circles until the gelding was calm again.

"Does he always do that?" Soraya asked as they walked across the stretch of grass to where Apollo stood, his head lowered and his sides heaving.

Tara grimaced. "Sometimes he's worse. Once he took me clear into the barn, and I had to duck to avoid getting knocked out. I wonder if it could have been the move from one training yard to another that's upset him. Maybe he's disoriented?"

Ben rejoined them. "Do you think you can help?"

"Let me go home and talk it over with Ty, and I'll get back to you as soon as I can," Amy promised as she gently smoothed Apollo's damp neck. She could feel all of the tension still bundled inside him. "I wouldn't want to push him any more today. Thanks for letting me see him – both sides of him."

As she turned away, Amy saw a brief look of disappointment flicker across Tara's face.

"That doesn't mean she can't help, it's just the way Amy works," Ben reassured Tara as he helped her down from the saddle.

"Scott's waiting for us by the Jeep. Didn't you want to see Storm before we leave?" Soraya suddenly reminded Amy.

"Daniel was grooming him in the barn earlier," Ben told them.

"Thanks," Amy smiled warmly, trying to make up for Soraya's frostiness. "I'll call you soon, I promise."

"Thanks, Amy. I really appreciate this," Tara called as the girls walked away.

Soraya and Amy headed up to the yard in silence. They found Scott leaning on the hood of his Jeep, flipping through a journal. "Do you mind if I try to find Daniel and Storm?" she asked. "I won't be long."

"Sure," Scott replied. "I need to head out in about ten minutes, though."

"OK." Amy hurried through the big double doors, aware that Soraya was trailing silently behind her. The barn was large and airy, and Amy's footsteps rang out as she strode down the centre aisle. She would have loved to have time to stop and stroke the noses of all the horses that were watching her with their ears pricked. Amy had to force herself to continue to the end of the spotless barn, inhaling the sweet mixture of sawdust and hay.

When she reached Storm's stall, Soraya called out from halfway down the aisle, "I'm going to say hello to the rest of the horses."

Amy shrugged and pulled back the sliding door into Storm's stall. The grey gelding was tethered to a ring in the back wall.

He swung his head around at the sound of Amy's footsteps and nickered gently.

Amy placed her hand on Storm's hindquarters so as not to startle him as she walked up to his head. He pushed his damp nose into her hands and she rubbed his forehead. "Hello, boy," she said softly. "You look as if you're being treated very well."

"I'm glad you think so," said a familiar voice. Daniel walked into the stall with an armful of tack.

"I should have known you'd be lurking nearby." Amy smiled.

"Of course. I love to overhear compliments on my grooming. Actually, Ben told me you were coming, so I gave Storm a little extra attention," Daniel said.

"He looks wonderful," Amy told him, taking the bridle out of his hands. She slipped the halter over Storm's neck while she put the bridle on.

"Thanks." Daniel's reply was muffled as he reached under Storm's stomach for the girth. "He's coming along well. We're off to another show next week."

Amy untied Storm and led him down the long aisle of the barn and out into the sunshine. Daniel checked the girth again before leading Storm to the mounting block, reaching up casually to smooth his forelock. Amy felt a real sense of pleasure as she looked at them. She would always feel a slight tinge of regret that she no longer owned Storm, but if she had the chance, she would do it all over again. Daniel could give the talented gelding all of the opportunities that Amy would never have had the time for.

Daniel's eyes met Amy's, and they were full of gratitude.

Amy smiled in understanding. "I'm pretty sure I'll be back soon, to see Apollo," she said.

"Maybe then you'll have time to ride Storm," Daniel suggested.

"I'd like that," said Amy. She gave Storm one last pat and watched the gelding walk confidently out of the yard with his ears pricked forward.

"All set?" Scott asked.

"Yep," Amy replied, glancing at Soraya, who was already sitting in the back of the Jeep. Her friend was twisting a strand of black hair around her finger and staring out the window. Amy sighed inwardly and got in beside Scott.

"Did you get a good sense of Apollo?" asked the vet as he started up the engine.

"Yes, thanks," Amy said, forgetting Soraya's mood as she began to describe what had happened with Apollo and ask Scott's opinion of his strange behaviour.

Scott dropped off Amy and Soraya. Before turning the Jeep around, he rolled down his window. "Can you tell Lou that I'll call her later? I don't have time to come in right now," he explained. Amy nodded, waving alongside Soraya as he pulled away.

They both headed to Lou's office and found her busily typing on her laptop. Amy passed on Scott's message and then glanced at the assorted envelopes strewn across the desk. "What's going on?"

Lou ran her fingers through her hair. "Replies to our save-the-date cards," she said. "Would you believe this many people have written back?" She waved her hand over the pile. "We haven't even sent out the formal invitations yet."

"Have you heard from everyone?" Soraya asked.

"No," Lou said. "But there are thirty replies here, and I'm sending out more save-the-date cards now that we've put a deposit down on a larger tent."

Soraya nodded. "Do you mind if I use the phone?"

"Sure," Lou said, rummaging around on her desk for the handset.

"It's OK," Soraya said. "I'll use the one in the kitchen."

"Do you need any help?" Amy asked when Soraya had left.

"Thanks for the offer," Lou smiled. "I've been here all morning and haven't come up for air yet! I'm setting up a database for all of the addresses and replies. It should make the whole thing more manageable." She pushed back her chair and stretched her hands above her head. "It's a one-person job, I'm afraid, but I'd love a cup of coffee if you're making one."

"No problem," Amy said.

She went down the hall into the kitchen where Soraya was flicking a tea towel at the edge of the table. "Coffee?" Amy offered, reaching into the cupboard for cups.

"No, thanks. It's too hot for coffee," Soraya answered abruptly. "Besides, I called my mom and she's on her way over to pick me up."

Amy felt baffled. Normally, Soraya would have wanted to stay and help out for a while. "Why are you going so soon?"

Soraya shrugged. She sat down at the table and plucked at a thread on the tablecloth before saying, "It didn't take Ben long to hook up with someone."

"I'm not sure he's hooked up. I don't think Ben moves that fast!" Amy joked.

"It's not funny. You just don't get it!" Soraya's voice broke and she took a deep breath. "It seems that every boy I know ends up liking someone else better."

Amy stared at her, hardly able to believe that this was her best friend talking. "Soraya, Ben liked you, but you were with Matt. You can't blame him for maybe liking someone else now."

"But look at Matt and Ashley!" Soraya retorted.

"What about Matt and Ashley? There is no Matt and Ashley!" Amy declared. "You know that Matt doesn't like Ashley any more. If he did, he would still be going out with her." She paused. "Listen, we all know what Ashley's like. You've only got to look at how her mother pushes her to know she's got some real issues. That's why Matt is being patient with her and, to be honest, I think you should be proud that he is still able to care about someone who is as difficult as she is."

Soraya pushed her chair back with a loud scraping noise and stood up. There was a horrified expression on her face. "What are you saying, Amy?"

Amy stared at her, lost for words.

Soraya didn't wait for a reply. "I can't believe you're taking Ashley's side. I'm your best friend!" She narrowed her eyes.

"But maybe now that Joni's here, I'm not as important to you, either," Soraya fumed. "And there's no way I could ever compete with the horses. Everyone knows they always come first! I don't know why I bother." Soraya looked Amy in the eye and shook her head. Then she grabbed her jacket and tore out of the room.

Chapter Five

Amy stayed where she was, frozen to the spot. She knew that she should follow Soraya and try to work things out with her before she left, but it was the last thing she felt like doing. She didn't know what to say that Soraya wouldn't distort into something else.

She finally forced herself to walk out to the yard and had mixed feelings when she saw Soraya already driving away in her mother's car. Although Amy didn't want bad feelings between them, she was so annoyed with Soraya that she wondered if some breathing space was what they both needed just now. They weren't on the same wavelength lately. She couldn't believe her best friend so clearly resented her dedication to Heartland. And that she would misinterpret Amy's opinion of Matt and Ashley's tenuous friendship.

Shrugging, Amy decided to try to forget what had just happened and concentrate instead on catching up with some yard work. Now that Venture had gone, she could disinfect his stall. Even though the big gelding hadn't been suffering from any sort of infection, it was important that there be no risk at all to incoming horses.

As she was filling up a bucket with water, she heard the sound of a car followed by a double beep of a horn. For a moment, Amy thought it was Soraya coming back, but when she looked up, she saw a small red car that she didn't recognize.

She broke into a wide smile when it stopped and Joni stepped out of the driver's side.

"What do you think?" Joni asked proudly.

Amy circled the car, which was old but in good condition. "It's terrific," she told her.

"I just wanted to stop by and show it off," said Joni, beaming. She ran her hand over the paint on the door. "It needs a little touching up, but mechanically it's really sound." She glanced up at Amy and frowned. "Is everything OK?"

Amy opened her mouth to explain that she had had a falling-out with Soraya, but then changed her mind. She would feel disloyal complaining about Soraya to Joni, especially since Soraya was acting so out of character. She didn't want to give Joni the wrong impression of her best friend.

"I guess I'm feeling a bit low with Venture gone," she said instead. "I thought I'd keep myself busy."

"Nobody would guess!" Joni laughed, looking at Amy's oversize rubber gloves and the still-dripping sponge in her hand.

Amy shrugged ruefully. "I was just getting started on Venture's stall. But I think I might end up doing the whole barn."

Joni shook her head. "You know, you exhibit several tell-tale signs of a workaholic. You're the one who told me that Venture leaving was just a sign that we've been doing our job properly."

Amy forced a smile, knowing that the reason she would be working flat out today was not to forget about Venture but to try not to think about her argument with Soraya.

* * *

Over Sunday lunch the next day, Amy and Ty discussed Apollo with Jack and Joni. Lou had gone out with Scott, so it was just the four of them.

"Have you decided if you're going to take him on?" Jack asked as he carried a bowl of steaming chilli con carne to the table.

"I think it might be best to work with Apollo in his own yard," Amy said. "That's where Tara wants to take him on the trails, so it makes sense."

Jack's forehead creased with a frown. "Do you think he might be dangerous?"

"Not at all," Amy said quickly, lowering her fork. "When I was watching him act up, there was no malice in his expression at all. He was clearly terrified of something. When he eventually bucked, it was obvious that he didn't want to hurt Tara, but he desperately wanted her to know that he didn't want to go into the field."

"It sounds more emotional than behavioural," Ty said thoughtfully.

"That's what I think," Amy agreed.

They were interrupted by the sound of Ty's cellphone ringing. "Sorry," he apologized as he pulled it out of his pocket. "It's my dad," he said, sounding puzzled as he read the caller ID. "I'll just take it outside." He pushed his chair away from the table and walked out of the room. "Hi, Dad. Is everything OK?" he asked, the screen door slamming behind him.

They all fell silent as the muffled sound of conversation filtered through the door. The moment Ty walked back into the room, Amy questioned, "Did something happen?"

He looked stunned. "I'm not sure," he said slowly. "Dad's supposed to be on this important job, driving from Pennsylvania to Georgia, but he said he needs to stop off here. He wouldn't explain why, just asked if we would be around to meet him."

"Didn't he say anything else?" Amy asked.

Ty shook his head. "He said that he'd explain everything when he got here." Ty started pacing the length of the kitchen. "He sounded stressed out. I hope he hasn't been laid off after all."

He barely touched the rest of his meal but kept glancing towards the door, even though Brad had said it would be nearly an hour before he would arrive. Amy could understand his unease – one family dinner couldn't have changed Brad's feelings about Ty's work so much that he'd want to drop by for a friendly visit. Something must be very wrong.

"Why don't you both go outside and wait?" Jack suggested finally. "Joni and I can clear up."

"Thanks, guys." Amy shot them both a grateful look and pushed back her chair. Ty said nothing as he put down his fork and left the table.

"Didn't your dad give you any idea what was wrong?" Amy asked Ty once they were out in the bright sunshine.

Ty shook his head. "This job is more important to him than anything else, Amy, and his new bosses have put him on a tight schedule. It seems like he's already running late. He left almost a week ago. I can't think of any reason why he would waste time making a detour here."

47

They had climbed on to the rail of the paddock fence, where they had a clear view of the drive leading up to Heartland. Amy slipped her arm through Ty's and felt the tension in his clenched muscles. "It will be OK," she offered, not knowing what else to say to reassure him. Ty nodded, but his eyes were fixed on the gravel road. Amy could feel the heat rising up from the ground. It was one of the hottest stretches she could remember for the time of year. They sat in silence for a while until a dust cloud appeared in the distance on the road.

"That could be him," said Ty, jumping down and shading his eyes.

Within a few minutes, they heard the clanking of a heavy vehicle, and soon a long, double-decker livestock carrier pulled steadily up the drive towards them. Brad was sitting in the driver's seat, and Amy caught a glimpse of his grim expression beneath his baseball cap as he drove past them into the yard.

"Is your dad transporting cattle?" Amy asked.

Ty didn't answer; he was already running after the truck. Amy hurried after him, and they were waiting to greet Brad when he jumped down from the cab.

"What's going on, Dad?" Ty demanded at once.

Brad took his hat off and wiped his arm across his forehead. His eyes looked troubled. "I need you to check my load over," he told them as he walked along the side of the truck.

Amy and Ty frowned at each other before jogging after Brad. "What do you have on board?" Ty called. "Cows? Sheep?"

The response was short and clipped. "Horses."

"Horses?" Amy stared in horror at the double-decker, feeling her heart sink. "Why do you have horses in there?" she stammered.

Brad began sliding the bolts at the back of the truck. "I didn't know what was in here when I turned up to drive the truck. It doesn't even belong to my company. When I stopped for lunch, I had a look through a slat in the side. I was as surprised as anyone that there were horses inside. I mean, I'd have thought they'd make more noise or move around, so I wondered if they were in a bad way. Two of them were lying down, and I figured they might need water or something."

"But this truck isn't suitable for horses!" Amy exclaimed, feeling breathless with shock. "It's for cattle." She swept her eyes over the long wooden-slatted vehicle, noting the lack of proper ventilation and the low ceiling height. "I don't even think it's legal!" She couldn't help a note of anger creeping into her voice, and Ty laid a warning hand on her arm.

"It doesn't have anything to do with me," Brad said defensively, turning around to meet her angry stare. "I just turned up at the auction house in Pennsylvania and was told to deliver them to a second auction house in Georgia. I had to wait days before the load was ready, so I lost any spare time I had. I've only been on the road six hours, and I'm supposed to be there tonight." He glanced at Ty. "Can you do anything? I mean, I need them to be OK when I get there, so maybe you could give them some water and something to eat?"

Ty's hand briefly tightened on Amy's arm before he said, "We'll try our best." He glanced with a silent plea at Amy. She swallowed hard and nodded.

49

"I'll go and get Jack and Joni," Ty said, and sprinted off towards the house.

Amy could already feel her stomach churning at the thought of what they might find in the truck. She looked at Brad. "I'm going to need your help to get the ramp down so I can lead them out."

Brad held up his hands and backed away. "Now, just hang on," he told her. "The reason I came here was for you to give them some food and water or whatever, and then for me to be back on my way. You don't need to unload them for that. Can't you just take some buckets in for them?"

Amy swallowed her rising impatience. "We have to open up the truck," she insisted quietly. "Let me have a better look, and then we can decide what to do, OK?" Without waiting for permission, she moved forward and began to tug on the remaining bolts.

Brad came forward to help her as she struggled with the heavy ramp. As it creaked down, Amy was hit by a wave of heat escaping from the truck. She blinked her eyes several times to try and adjust to the dark as she peered inside the trailer. The smell was overwhelming. The truck had obviously been used to carry cattle, without being properly cleaned out afterwards. Amy felt her stomach turn over, and she lifted her hand to cover her nose and mouth. She blinked again and began to make out various shapes inside the truck.

"I'll go get some halters," said a voice beside her. Amy hadn't even noticed that Joni had joined them, and she nodded automatically, unable to tear her eyes away from the trailer.

Jack and Ty came to stand on either side of her. "As soon as Joni comes back, we'll lead them out one by one," Jack said. "We'll have to go carefully. You don't know what state they'll be in, and we don't want to put ourselves in danger."

Amy's heart began to pound. "What do you mean?"

"They could be panicked or in shock, which will make them stressed out and unpredictable. Did Ty say that two of them are lying down?" Jack looked at Brad with his eyebrows raised.

Brad rubbed his hand over the back of his neck and nodded. "It looked as if at least two of them were down, but it was difficult to make out. Maybe they're up now."

"Do you know how many are in there?" Amy asked.

Brad shook his head as Joni arrived back, clutching a handful of halters and lead ropes. "Here," she panted.

"It's going to be best if we don't all go in at once. We don't want to startle them," Jack said.

Amy licked her dry lips. "I'll go."

"Me, too," said Ty, putting his foot on the ramp. As they began to walk up the slope, Amy was aware that his breath was quick and shallow.

They hesitated at the top of the ramp, waiting for their eyesight to adjust to the gloom. Amy wiped her sticky hands on her jeans. One of the horses let out a loud, frightened snort, and when she peered in the direction of the sound, she made out two glinting eyes staring in her direction. "I'm going in," she said.

"I'm right beside you," Ty said grimly.

Amy started to inch over the wooden floor towards the horse. "Steady there," she murmured.

The horse let out another snort and stepped backwards. Amy's eyes were getting used to the light by now, and she could make out the inside of the truck more clearly.

"Oh, Ty," she whispered. Her throat tightened, and she felt a rush of nausea as the smell of ammonia ached through her nose and mouth. Swallowing hard, Amy swept her gaze over the horses huddled miserably together. "How could anyone do this?"

Ty shook his head wordlessly as he joined her, his head ducked to avoid the low wooden ceiling. His eyes swept unblinkingly over the still figures. Amy thought she could count eight horses, all obviously in a state of shock. Their heads were hung down away from the roof, and most of them didn't even look up when Amy and Ty walked over.

The horse that Amy had first caught sight of was the only one moving. It was smaller than the others, a light bay of about fourteen hands. His eyes were wide, the whites blazing with fear as he focused on Amy.

Amy took a deep breath. "We should get him out first," she said, nodding towards the bay, which didn't look any older than a yearling. He had a wild, frightened look to his eyes, and Amy was terrified that at any moment he might rear and crack his head on the treacherously low ceiling.

Ty nodded. "Steady, boy." He spoke soothingly as the roan horse snorted and skidded backwards into a chestnut gelding. The gelding staggered, his eyes rolling, and Amy was suddenly afraid that panic might break out. But the horses all seemed to be subdued by the appalling conditions, unable to muster the energy to fight their fear. With her heart racing, Amy stepped forward to slip her arms around the colt's warm neck. She tangled her hand in his thick mane and murmured encouragingly. The colt tried to shake her off, but Amy maintained her grasp.

"Nice work," Ty said as he clipped on the halter. He rubbed the yearling's nose before clicking his tongue to urge him forward.

The colt refused to move. "He's terrified," Amy said. "He doesn't understand that we're here to help him."

"Can you get a halter on the chestnut and lead him out?" Ty asked, his voice taut with strain. "Maybe the young one will follow."

Amy reached out to let the gelding sniff at her hand. The chestnut just rested his lips against her fingers. It was as if he didn't even have the energy to look away. Amy gently pulled the halter over his ears before clicking to him to walk on. For one heart-stopping moment, she didn't think that the gelding was going to move, either. Then, slowly, the chestnut shuffled forward. Amy's chest was tight with tension, and she could see the outline of his ribcage and spine when he stepped into the light. As they passed the yearling, Amy heard his small hooves scramble after them.

"Nice and slow," Ty warned.

Joni, Jack and Brad were waiting with anxious expressions as the gelding hesitantly angled his way down the ramp. Wordlessly, Amy handed over the chestnut to Joni and took another halter from her.

"Do you want me to go in?" Joni asked, placing her hand on Amy's arm.

Amy shook her head, unconsciously twisting the halter in her hands until her knuckles were white. "I think they should be put in the shade until Scott gets here," she said, her voice sounding strange to her ears. "Ty and I will get the rest of them out. If new people go in, it might freak them out more."

"Amy, may I use your cellphone to call Scott? I don't want to go up to the house in case you have problems getting any of the others out," Jack said.

Amy wordlessly handed over her phone before turning back to the trailer.

"Can I do anything?" Brad was standing awkwardly at the side of the truck, picking at a splinter of wood.

Amy felt a surge of anger and frustration at his question. *You could have prevented this!* she wanted to scream. Instead, she shook her head and walked back up the ramp.

"You can help Joni lead the horses down to the closest paddock. There are plenty of trees for shade there," she heard Ty tell his dad as he hurried after her.

The moment she stepped into the truck, Amy's attention was taken by a palomino pressed up against the wall. The mare's head was hanging lower than the others, and she had two nasty cuts on her forehead that were caked with blood. Amy thought she saw the horse's knees wavering. "Ty, help me! This one's hit her head on the roof!" she cried as she tried to support the palomino.

Ty joined her on the other side of the mare. "It looks as if she's been bitten by one of the other horses, too," he said, his fingers grazing over a neck wound.

Amy looped a lead rope behind the horse's ears to avoid a halter rubbing against her wounds. She stepped ahead and Ty stayed at the mare's side. Slowly they inched their way towards the ramp. "Good girl, nearly there," Amy said over and over, rubbing the palomino's muzzle.

"Careful!" Ty called as they began to come down the ramp. The palomino's hoof slid against the metal, and Ty's arms swung around her neck. Her legs buckled and Amy put her back against the mare's chest as the horse pitched forward. Her hooves clattered as she regained her balance, but Amy stayed in front of her as support until the mare's front legs were on firm ground. When Amy stood up, Joni took hold of the mare's lead.

"Poor girl," Joni whispered when she saw the blood staining the golden coat.

Amy nodded, unable to speak. She barely noticed Ty take hold of her hand as they made their way up the ramp again.

Only three of the remaining horses were still standing. They were grouped closely together in the shadows at the back. Ty squeezed Amy's hand before slipping a halter over a bay mare, leaving Amy to get the black gelding that was next to her. Amy put her head close to the gelding's and reached up to smooth his forelock. "Please walk," she whispered, her throat dry and stinging. "Just a short walk and you'll be out of here." The black gelding sighed heavily and turned away, facing the opposite direction of the ramp. Amy felt helpless. She reached out and tapped the black on his shoulder. "C'mon, boy, walk," she urged. "This way." She poked him behind his bloated belly until he stumbled around and followed her.

Amy was shocked at how sunken the animal's eyes were as she led him into the light. The third horse, a grey mare, came listlessly after them.

They picked their way down the ramp, and even though the grey mare was loose, she was too tired to do anything other than stand, trembling, alongside the palomino.

"She's too weak to walk down to the ring," Joni said as Amy looked at the golden mare. She rubbed the mare gently on the forehead before taking the black gelding's lead rope out of Amy's hand. Joni's eyes were red-rimmed, but Amy felt too exhausted to do anything other than exchange a look full of shared anguish with her.

Brad cleared his throat. "I can take the black horse down to the schooling ring so you can stay with this one." He nodded at the palomino.

Joni handed him the lead rope before returning to the palomino and gently running her hands through the mare's mane.

"I called Scott and Lou. They're on their way," Jack told them. He glanced at Amy and his eyes narrowed. "How many more to come out?"

"Just the two lying down," Amy said, taking the handkerchief from his hand and blowing her nose.

"I'm coming in with you this time," Jack said firmly.

Amy headed back up the ramp. She made her way through the wet, stinking straw to the back of the trailer with Jack beside her. They both crouched down next to the first horse they came to, a dark bay gelding. Amy could see the shape of every rib, and her stomach lurched as she looked at the gash stretching from one of the horse's ears to the other. The horse had clearly cracked his head on the roof and collapsed. Now his brown eyes were clouded, and he stared out at nothing. When Amy saw Jack slowly shaking his head, she knew there was nothing anyone could do for this horse any more.

"I'm so sorry, boy," Amy whispered, and gently ran her hand along the horse's neck. She felt her grandfather's hand on her shoulder as she twisted her fingers in the matted black mane, and then she felt her eyes fill with futile tears.

Chapter Six

Amy swallowed hard and lifted her head as Ty came towards them. He kneeled down and rested his hand briefly on the gelding's shoulder. Amy noticed a muscle twitch in his jaw before he looked at her.

He shook his head and sighed before touching Amy on the arm. "I know it's the last thing you feel like doing, but we have to move on. We need to concentrate on the others."

"Ty's right." Jack's voice was raw with anger and grief as he helped Amy to stand. She gave one last sympathetic look at the gelding before drawing a deep, shaky breath and turning her attention to the other horse – an old chestnut mare that was lying with her front legs tucked underneath her chest, her nose resting on the soiled straw. The horse's shoulder twitched when Amy touched her neck to find a pulse. She tried to encourage the mare to stand, but the horse just looked at her through listless eyes.

Ty frowned. "I don't think we'll get her out."

"Scott will be here any minute. He'll be able to see to her then. I think we should look at the others," Jack agreed.

Amy nodded and gave the mare's neck one final stroke before rising to her feet, aware of an incredible anger building in her.

Out in the yard, it was obvious that the palomino could hardly stand. Joni was waving her hands around the mare's face, and Amy soon realized it was to deter the cluster of flies drawn by the open wounds.

Brad stepped forward, a baffled expression on his face. "Will it take you long to help them?" he asked gruffly, his question directed at Jack. "I'm going to be really pushed for time."

Amy could hardly believe what she was hearing.

"We need to wait for the vet," Jack replied simply.

"Hope he gets here soon." Brad shifted his weight from one foot to the other. "This is a big contract for my new bosses…" He paused and swallowed. "I can't mess it up."

"You can't mess it up," Amy repeated slowly under her breath, her fingers clenching and digging into her palms.

Ty, standing next to Jack, shot Amy a warning look.

"Of course I don't want to leave until they're OK to travel," Brad added. "If you tell me where your tap is, I'll help you carry out some buckets of water."

Blood pounded in Amy's ears, and she felt the burning in her chest explode. "Those horses are never getting back on that trailer. You'll be signing their death warrant," she yelled. "How can your bosses make a contract with an auction house that transports their horses in vehicles like that?" She jabbed her hand towards the trailer.

Before Brad could respond, Ty walked across and put his hand on Amy's arm. "Maybe we should discuss this later on," he suggested quietly. "Don't forget, Dad didn't load the horses, he was just hired to drive them. The main thing is that he brought the horses to us instead of continuing to drive. We just have to concentrate on trying to save them. OK?"

Amy looked at Ty and felt a little of her anger ebb away.

"Trying to save them?" Brad questioned. But nobody answered; their attention was caught by Scott's Jeep pulling up outside the house. Jack immediately headed across the yard, and Amy hurried after him.

By the time they reached the Jeep, Scott was already pulling his medical kit from the back. Lou jumped out and surveyed the yard, taking in the trailer and the grave expressions on all their faces. "What's going on?" she asked in a bewildered tone.

"Ty's dad was transporting a load of horses and he brought them here when he realized there was a problem." Amy glanced at Scott. "It's awful." Her voice broke as she began to describe what they had discovered. "We didn't want to do anything until you saw them. They all appear to be in shock, and one of them –" she fought to get the words out – "one of them is ... dead."

Lou held her hand to her mouth and her face turned pale.

"How many are there?" Scott asked, his expression stony.

"Seven still alive," Jack said. "The palomino over there is doing badly, and there's a mare still inside. We couldn't get her to stand."

Scott broke into a run, and when he reached the truck he climbed straight up the ramp with Ty. They were in the trailer for a matter of moments before reappearing and joining Amy.

Scott shook his head briefly. "I'll take a look at the other horses first," he said, his voice grim. "Where are they?"

"In the paddock," Amy told him.

"I'll go with you," Joni said. Her hands trembled as she

handed the palomino's lead rope to Brad. He stood at the end of the rope with an uncertain expression on his face.

Scott jogged towards the ring with Joni and Jack.

"Is there anything I can do?" Lou asked Amy, her blue eyes wide with shock.

"Can you go to the barn and get some of the flower remedies together?" Amy asked.

"Which ones?"

"Rock Rose, Hawthorn, Olive and Rescue." Amy rattled off the remedies that sprang to mind for helping horses that were stressed and dehydrated. She gave Lou a grateful glance and turned to follow Scott, but Brad stopped her.

"Isn't he going to give this one an injection or something?" He nodded towards the palomino.

Amy looked at his puzzled expression. "He'll come back to see to her, but he needs to look at the others first," she said, pushing to the back of her mind the terrible thought that Scott was dealing with the ones that he had the best chance of saving.

"Can you stay with the mare? We won't be long," Amy told him.

Brad glanced at the palomino and opened his mouth as if he were about to say something. Then he nodded his head.

The remaining five horses were standing quietly under the shade of the trees. Scott was examining each one while Jack and Joni held them.

"Amy." Scott turned to face her. "It's pretty bad. They're all suffering from dehydration and stress, which is hardly surprising. Two of them –" he nodded at the bay and the black – "are in the initial stages of heatstroke, so we need to move fast if we're going to save them."

"What do you need us to do?"

Scott wiped his sleeve across his forehead. "I need to get these two up to the stable block and set up an IV line of electrolytes. The other three can stay here in the shade. I need you to give them this paste on their tongues." He handed Amy three packages. "It contains oral electrolytes. Then you can sponge them down with cool water – not too cold."

Amy nodded. She'd often hosed down horses after intense summer workouts, but it had never been a life-and-death situation. "Lou's up in the barn. Can you tell her we need buckets of water and sponges?"

"Will do." Scott took hold of the bay mare's halter and gently persuaded her to walk with him. Jack led the black. As Amy began to tear open the packets, there was the sound of footsteps pounding towards her.

Brad was racing towards them, waving his cap in the air. "You've got to come quickly," he called. He skidded to a stop just in front of Amy, his face pale beneath his tan. "The horse has gone down," he panted. "I tried to keep it standing up, but its legs just buckled. It's lying on the ground now, and it won't move."

"We'll get up to her as soon as we can, but we need to help these horses first," Amy told him, every word wrenched from her throat.

"What can I do to help her? She's just lying there," Brad said again, dismay in his eyes.

"Just let her know you're there," Amy said softly.

Brad turned away, his shoulders hunched, as Amy handed the packets of oral electrolytes to Ty and Joni. Amy approached the bay colt, who was standing quietly, his nose almost touching the fence. He swung his head around and blew suspiciously at the tube in her hands.

"It's to make you better," Amy told him. The yearling snorted again and flattened his ears as she took hold of his halter. He stepped back, pulling against her, but Amy held him firmly and squeezed the paste into the corner of his mouth. She held his head for a second longer to make sure that he had swallowed before letting go. The colt nodded his head up and down and chewed with an open mouth, trying to get rid of the unfamiliar taste.

"Look at this!" Joni suddenly exclaimed from beside the chestnut gelding. Amy left the yearling and quickly joined her. She winced at the deep wounds Joni was pointing to on the quarters and rump of the chestnut. The shape of the cuts suggested they weren't made by teeth or hooves, which meant they couldn't have been caused by the other horses.

"This one has them, too," Ty called. He stroked the neck of the grey and shook his head. "I'm guessing the people who loaded them must have had trouble getting them in with that low ceiling." His green eyes flared with disgust. "I've seen those marks once before, and that was from an electric cattle prod."

Joni gasped and Amy felt her stomach churn as she hurried

to check over the yearling. Of all the horses, he seemed to be in the best condition. When Amy ran her hands over his flanks, checking for injuries, she felt a light touch on the top of her head. The yearling had turned around and was snuffling at her hair just like Sundance did when he was in a good mood. Amy felt a sudden surge of protective anger. He was so young.

She glanced up to see Jack and Lou walking across the arena, carrying black buckets. Lou set two of them down in front of Amy, while Jack carried his across to Joni and Ty. Lou looked at each of the horses. "How are they?"

"They all took the electrolytes, but it's too soon to tell if they'll have an effect," Amy said. "Did you bring the remedies?"

"Yes, here they are," said Lou, fishing several small brown glass bottles out of her pocket.

"I think we should try and get them to lick Rescue Remedy off our hands before we sponge them down," Amy decided.

"I'll help Joni," Lou offered, her voice trembling slightly.

Amy noticed that Jack was already squeezing a sponge over the grey. She walked across the ring and squeezed a few drops of Rescue Remedy into Ty's outstretched hand. Amy felt some of the tension leave her chest as the grey tentatively began to lick Ty's palm. Ty lifted his eyes to give Amy a slight smile before grabbing a sponge and returning his attention to the mare.

When Amy joined Joni, she noticed the stable girl's hand tremble as she dropped the Rescue Remedy on to it. The chestnut gelding's head drooped low, and Amy watched as Joni crouched down and coaxed him to lick the remedy by murmuring words of encouragement and tickling his muzzle.

As soon as the chestnut began to move his lips over Joni's hand, Amy returned to the colt. His ears flickered in her direction. "C'mon, boy. Your turn now," Amy urged. The yearling moved his soft nose over her hand, his whiskers tickling her gently. "Good boy," Amy said softly, running her hands down his neck and then dragging a bucket closer.

She started sponging the colt with water. She wondered if she should tether him to the fence, but he stood calmly with his eyes half closed as she squeezed the cool water over his legs.

Amy had used up nearly all the water in her bucket when Scott rejoined her.

"Things are looking better here," he said.

Amy straightened up and wiped her arm across her forehead. It was still hot, even in the shade. "How are the bay and the black?" she asked.

"They're pretty subdued at the moment, which you'd expect. All we can do now is wait." He narrowed his eyes. "I'm sorry, Amy, but when I checked the mare in the truck again, she had died." He ran his fingers through his hair and gave Amy a knowing glance. "I examined the palomino, too." He paused, and when he spoke again, his voice was flat. "Are you up to helping me?"

Amy's stomach tightened, but she nodded with determination. As she turned to follow Scott, Ty called across, "Will these guys be OK to be left once we've finished sponging them down?"

"Just for a while, yes," Scott called back. "Someone should keep an eye on them to make sure they don't roll. And they should be sponged every twenty minutes or so."

Amy took one more look at the yearling, who was watching her with his ears pricked, before hurrying with Scott back to the yard.

Brad was sitting cross-legged on the ground next to the palomino, stroking her neck. He had taken his shirt from around his waist and placed it under the mare's head. Amy was surprised to see this hopeless gesture of comfort from Ty's dad.

Brad looked up as they approached. "Have you been able to save the others?" he asked hoarsely.

"I hope so," said Scott. "We'll move them to the barn later and see if they'll take a soft bran mash before we leave them for the night."

Brad frowned and stood up. "I hate to be the bad guy, but I'm not sure my bosses will allow that. I'm going to have to phone them and let them know what's happening. They might want to make me finish the trip."

Amy looked at him with horror. "How can you even think about putting them back into that trailer?" she gasped. She searched Brad Baldwin's face for some comprehension of the unfolding tragedy. She didn't even notice the others walk back into the yard.

Brad looked her in the eye. "It's my job, Amy," he said helplessly.

Jack cleared his throat. "If your bosses think that they're going to load these animals back into that death trap, then they're going to have a fight on their hands."

Amy shot her grandfather a grateful glance. She crouched

down beside the palomino's head and began to rub gently between the mare's eyes.

"Those horses aren't up to travelling anywhere today," Scott told Brad as he knelt down and opened his bag. His face was pale as he said, "She's got one of the worst cases of heatstroke I've ever seen. Her vital organs are all shutting down. I think it's best to get this over with."

Amy felt as if everything were happening in slow motion. As she gazed into the mare's pain-filled eyes, she could see Scott check her pulse again, reach in his bag, and pull out a bolt pistol.

"Hey, wait a minute," Brad objected, walking forward. "You can't just shoot it."

"Look, Dad." Ty left Jack's side and reached out to put a hand on his father's arm. "Why don't you go in and get yourself something to drink? You've done a great job here so far."

Brad stared at Ty as if he suddenly didn't know who he was. "What do you mean 'great job'? Don't talk to me like I'm some kid," Brad scolded. But Ty didn't pull away.

"It's the kindest thing we can do for her. She's suffering." Ty's voice was even and honest. "She's going to die. If we leave her here, it will be a very painful death."

Brad shook his head as if he couldn't accept what Ty was saying. The palomino groaned again and closed her eyes. Brad flinched. "I'm staying," he said stubbornly. "I'm not leaving her now." He dropped down on the ground beside the palomino and placed his hand gently on her cheek.

"Amy." Scott looked directly at her, his eyes sympathetic.

"Can you help Brad hold her head for me?"

Amy couldn't speak. Her mouth was completely dry, but she knew what Ty had said was true. It was the one last act of kindness that could be shown towards her. *I wonder if she's known any other in her life*, Amy thought, brushing her hand lightly down the mare's nose before taking hold of the lead line.

Her heart thudded painfully as Scott placed the bolt pistol against the palomino's forehead. The mare's eyelids flickered open and then shut again as she let out a heavy sigh. Amy looked up at Brad's pale face and glanced away as Scott pulled the trigger. There was a muffled thud, the mare jerked just once, and then everything was still.

Chapter Seven

Brad pushed himself to his feet and walked away. Amy looked up to see Lou wiping tears off her cheeks. She felt strong arms helping her stand, and her grandpa hugged her briefly. "It'll be OK," he murmured into her hair.

Lou blinked hard. "There's nothing else to do here now. I think we should go inside." She turned and hurried towards the house.

"Do you have something you can use to cover her?" Scott asked, nodding at the palomino's body. "I can call for the bodies to be picked up."

"There's a tarp in the barn. I'll go get it," Jack said gruffly.

Ty was staring after Brad. Amy could see uncertainty etched on his face.

"You should go talk to him," she said softly.

Ty turned to her, shaking his head. "I didn't think my dad would react like that."

"He wanted to do what was right. He really did," Amy said. "You should see how he is."

Ty shrugged and walked across to where Brad was leaning on the fence, staring into the paddock. Amy gave the mare's still body a final glance before heading into the house.

She sank down on to a chair in the kitchen and rested her head on the table. Lou silently got glasses out of the cupboard. The normal day-to-day noises sounded alien to Amy's ears. She closed her eyes, but immediately the image of the suffering horses poured into her head, and she could still smell the stench of the truck.

Amy raised her head when she heard Joni come into the kitchen. "Ty said he'd keep an eye on the three in the paddock," she explained. "He also told me about the palomino. I'm not sure I can take any more."

Lou put glasses down in front of them both.

"At least I disinfected the stalls yesterday," Amy remarked, forcing herself to sound businesslike. "That means all we have to do is bed them down with straw."

"I'll help you do that," Joni offered. She sat down opposite Amy and began pleating the edge of the tablecloth. "I'll take any mindless chore right about now."

At that moment the door opened and Ty walked in with Brad. "We can check on the horses from the window," said Ty as they both sat down. "Dad and I need a little break."

Lou nodded and placed ice cubes into a large jug before carrying it across to the table.

Amy looked up and saw weariness in Brad's face – an expression so similar to his son's that Amy caught her breath. "It's not your fault," she blurted out. "I know I was angry, but I swear it wasn't with you. The horses must have been in an awful state before being loaded," she continued. "A six-hour journey – even in that trailer – wouldn't have affected healthy horses like that."

Brad nodded slowly. "I understand that you're going to need to keep the horses here. Ty explained it to me. But –" he paused – "I'm going to have to phone my bosses and let them know what's going on." He leaned back in his chair and frowned. "I'm just worried that they're going to insist that I continue the trip, and when I refuse…" His voice trailed away.

"Dad's convinced that they'll have grounds to fire him," Ty finished quietly as Scott walked into the room.

"I think you have an argument," Scott said. "You can start by pointing out to your employers that whoever loaded the horses on to the trailer broke the law."

Brad looked startled. "Are you sure?"

"It recently became illegal to transport horses in double-decker vehicles in Pennsylvania," Scott told him. "I just confirmed it with one of my colleagues."

Brad pushed his chair back and began to pace the kitchen floor. "So what do you think I should do? Report the auction house to the authorities?" He almost collided with Jack, who was coming in through the back door. Jack headed straight to the sink to wash his hands.

Scott cleared his throat. "That's up to you and your employers. The most important thing to us is that these horses are cared for."

"Maybe it was just a one-time thing. We don't even know that the auction house was to blame! It's just as likely that it was the owners of the horses." Brad ran a hand through his short black hair.

"You don't have to report the auction house, but you have to report the crime," Amy said decidedly as her grandfather came to sit beside her. "You have to. If the auction house isn't responsible, then the police can find out who is."

Jack put one hand on Amy's arm and gave it a reassuring squeeze. "Did you actually see who loaded the horses, Brad?" he asked.

"No, they were all on the trailer when I arrived. I just signed the papers for them and left."

"Well, we could start by looking at the papers," Ty suggested. "They might tell us who owns the horses, so at least we'd be able to help the auction house find who's responsible."

"That sounds like a good idea," Lou said. She stood up. "How about you go with your dad to get the documents from the truck, Ty?"

Amy pushed her chair back, feeling a rush of relief at the thought of some positive action. "And we'll go and bring the horses in while you're getting the papers."

It didn't take long for the five of them to prepare the stalls with deep beds of fresh straw. It was lucky they could make room for the unexpected visitors, since the weather was warm enough to turn out a couple of other residents for the night. Amy added Star of Bethlehem to the drinking water to help treat any remaining shock; then she joined Scott to check the two older horses while the others went to bring in the three from the paddock.

"How's he doing?" Amy asked, running her eyes over the black gelding, who was standing quietly at the back of the stall.

Scott pinched the horse's skin. "There's more elasticity now, which is a good sign," he said. "When horses get dehydrated, their skin tends to stay tensed when you tug on it, instead of relaxing flat again." He gave the gelding a final pat before going to the bay mare in the adjoining stall.

"Scott —" Amy hesitated — "do you think we could have done anything to save the horses that died? I keep thinking that if only I'd gone ahead and treated them before you arrived..." Her voice trailed off.

"Listen," Scott said, his eyes filled with sincerity. "You did everything you could. The ones we lost were past saving. And the other ones needed time to adjust after you got them out of the trailer. The important thing is that the rest have a chance of pulling through."

Amy nodded, but her heart still felt heavy as she watched Scott examine the mare, who was standing with her head low. The mare sniffed at her outstretched hand and then closed her eyes as Amy began to rub small, soothing circles into the top of her neck.

Scott crouched down to listen to the mare's heart rate. "It's still faster than I'd like," he said after a few moments.

"Why's that?" Brad's deep voice asked from behind them. He was standing alongside Ty, looking over the stall door. "We've got all the papers we could find in the truck," he added. He ran his dark brown eyes over the mare. "She's going to be all right, isn't she?"

Scott ran his hand down the mare's shoulder. "I hope so. When animals get dehydrated, their heart rate increases because there's less fluid in the blood vessels. It means that the heart has to pump the blood faster to achieve the same effect."

73

He patted the mare's back. "We've given them electrolytes to replace the salts and minerals that they've lost. The rest is up to them now."

Amy looked at the mare's sunken eyes and visible ribcage and knew that even if she pulled through, it would be a long road to recovery. She pressed a kiss on the mare's forehead. "You can do it," she whispered. The mare sighed again as Amy left the stall to join the others. They turned at the sound of hooves entering the barn to see Joni, Jack and Lou leading the three other horses.

Amy hurried forward to open the door to one of the stalls, and she smiled as Joni led the yearling in. As soon as his halter was off, the colt began exploring his stall, sniffing at the deep bed of straw.

"I think he's responding more quickly than the others," said Joni. She glanced at Amy. "If it's OK, I'll get started on the evening feeds now."

Amy glanced at her watch in surprise. "Is it that late?" Time had raced by since Brad had arrived.

Ty, Brad and Scott joined them to watch as the long-legged colt ran his lips over the rim of the water bucket.

"How could anyone let these horses suffer?" Ty wondered out loud.

Scott pulled off his gloves and rolled them up. "At least they're here now."

Amy felt her heart lift when Brad nodded his head, a determined expression passing over his face as he watched the yearling dip his nose into the bucket.

"The Pennsylvania law is supposed to prevent this," Scott added as he turned away from the stall.

"But it still happened," Amy said, feeling sickened.

"I'm really sorry, but I'm going to have to go," Scott said when they reached the kitchen door. "I'm behind on the rest of my calls. If you need me, call and I'll come straight back." He gave Lou a quick kiss goodbye and then glanced at Jack. "I've got a Polaroid camera in my Jeep. It might be a good idea if you took some photos of the horses and trailer. You don't know how much opposition you might be up against if you report the auction house or owners, and you're going to need all the evidence you can get."

"Yes, I think so, too," said Jack.

"I'll come out with you and get the camera," Ty volunteered, pushing his foot back into the boot he had just kicked off.

"Thanks for everything, Scott." Amy knew it had been as hard on him as anyone – no matter how professional he appeared, there was still a personal investment and a sense of loss. Scott gave her a tired smile before heading outside with Ty.

"Look at this!" Lou exclaimed. She was leaning on the kitchen table, looking at the pile of papers Brad had brought from the truck. Amy and her grandfather exchanged a quick, hopeful glance before joining her.

"What does it say?" Jack asked.

"It's an agreement between the owners of the horses and the auction house," Lou said, her voice rising with excitement. "It says that if the horses don't make their reserve price at the live auction, the sponsoring auction house will pay the reserve fee and keep the horses."

"So that means that the auction house owns the horses now?" Amy asked in surprise, leaning closer to read the creased piece of paper for herself.

"That's how I understand it!" Lou pointed at a paragraph of small type.

Jack reached over and pulled another piece of paper from the pile. He scanned it, then looked up. "This says the same thing. It's obviously an agreement with a different owner. It mentions just one horse."

"Read it out loud, Grandpa," Amy prompted, leaning to one side as Brad reached across to take the remaining stapled sheet of paper.

"'Light bay colt, thirteen months, to make fifteen-point-two hands.' That's all it says."

Amy's heart leaped at the mention of the yearling.

"Mine is for a grey mare, fourteen-point-three hands, and a chestnut gelding, fifteen hands," Lou read.

"Which means that there was at least one other owner for the remaining five," Amy said.

"Here you go," Brad put in, running his eyes down the paper. "Yes, I think this covers the other five." He showed Amy the descriptions.

"The three that are dead, the old black gelding, and the old bay mare." Amy shuddered. "How can people just not care what happens to their animals after they've sent them to auction?" she demanded incredulously. "So the reason that the auction house was sending them to the second auction in Georgia must have been to try to make a profit on the reserve price that they paid."

"Maybe they were giving them a chance to find good homes in a different state?" Brad suggested hopefully.

"More likely they were sending them to end up in a slaughterhouse somewhere," Amy retorted. "No horse in the condition they were in would be bought for riding. And they're probably worth more if they're sold for meat."

Brad's face fell, and Amy had to remind herself again that it wasn't his fault. He had done all he could.

At that moment, Ty walked back into the kitchen, holding a small clutch of Polaroids. Amy showed him the contracts that proved the horses belonged to the auction house while Jack made a fresh pot of coffee and Lou took a loaf of bread out of the cupboard.

Ty and Amy looked up from the documents when Brad pushed his chair back from the table with a scrape and walked across to stand by the window. He looked at his watch. "I'm going to have to call in now," he said. He pulled out his cellphone and punched in a number before turning to look out the window. From his opening words, Amy guessed that Brad had reached one of the secretaries. He began to explain that he'd been held up and then stopped mid-sentence. "They've put me on hold," he explained over his shoulder.

Suddenly, there was a raised voice at the other end of the phone. "I'm sorry," Brad cut in firmly. "Like I said, I've been held up." He listened for a moment before saying, "Look, I'll call again tomorrow with an update." He ended the call and looked around with a guilty expression. "Well, I've done it now," he said. "My boss was furious. He kept asking what the hold-up was about. I need to be one hundred per cent sure that the auction house was to blame before I make any accusations. It's not just my job on the line here."

"You did the right thing," Ty told him as Brad sat back down and took a gulp of his coffee. "You've just got to prove to your bosses that it was impossible for you to continue with your journey once you had discovered how sick the horses were. There must be some laws we can research, and then you can even say that you were protecting your firm's own interests! The auction house should never have allowed horses in that condition to go on such a long trip – and that's beside the fact that the double-decker carrier is illegal for horses."

Brad nodded uncertainly, and Amy wrapped her hands around her mug, praying that Brad's job would be spared and the auction house would be held responsible for the condition of the horses.

"I got Scott to sign the back of the Polaroids and write a statement confirming how sick the horses were," Ty continued, pulling a sheet of paper out of his jeans pocket.

Brad raised his eyebrows in Ty's direction, but he still seemed deep in thought.

"That was good thinking," said Lou, bringing a plate of sandwiches to the table. She picked up a Polaroid. "This is great evidence."

"What do I need to do next?" Brad asked, sitting back down at the table.

Although Amy hadn't thought she would be able to eat a thing, she was surprised to discover that she was actually quite hungry. She bit into a tuna sandwich while Ty told them his plan.

"I'll go with Dad tomorrow to the company headquarters. We can show them all the evidence that proves the horses were at risk. I'll be able to describe the state of the animals when they were unloaded and say that, in my opinion, most of them would have been dead on arrival if you had driven all the way to Georgia."

"That sounds sensible to me," Jack commented, leaning forward to take a sandwich. "And perhaps you can ask the company to make inquiries about rehoming those horses. After all, we need to figure out what happens to them now."

Amy glanced sideways at her grandfather and felt an icy chill despite the spring heat. She hadn't considered the fact that the auction house might still have a say over the horses' future. What if they insist the horses still go to Georgia? She tried to push down the panic rising inside her. *We won't let that happen*, she thought.

Brad Baldwin echoed her worst fears. "They might still want the horses sent on to Georgia to fulfil their end of the contract. To them, it's just a business deal." Then he looked directly at Amy, and her heart lifted when she saw the determination in his eyes. "But Ty and I will do our best to keep them here, that's for sure."

Amy hoped that Brad wouldn't lose his conviction. He had a trying battle ahead.

* * *

Ty left to take his dad home, and Amy slipped out into the fading light to find Joni. A sweet smell hit her nostrils as soon as she walked into the barn and she saw five buckets, all with a bran mash cooling in them. Joni was nowhere in sight, so Amy walked back out into the yard.

The tall, slender stable girl must have just come out from one of the stables. She was standing by the tap with her back to Amy, leaning over a bucket as it filled with water.

Amy watched her for a moment. "You didn't have to do all of the evening chores on your own – but thanks, it's a terrific help."

Joni turned round and gave a wan smile. Her eyes and nose were red from crying. "I've left Sundance and Jasmine out in the field for tonight. All of the horses have been fed except for the auction horses, and I've mucked out the stalls…" As her voice faded, she looked down at the bucket in her hand.

Amy reached out and took the bucket from the older girl's grip. "It's OK, I'll do the rest. You've done more than enough," she said. She knew just how Joni was feeling. *This is exactly how I used to react when horses were suffering*, she remembered. *I'd be in a panic to do anything and everything for them, as fast as possible, hoping that it might help.* Her thoughts slipped back to the fateful night when she had insisted that her mother drive beyond Teak's Hill to rescue Spartan. If only she had been patient and waited until the storm had passed. She hadn't been able to see beyond the horse's predicament to the bigger picture.

Amy dragged her attention back to Joni. "There's nothing else you can do for those horses," she told her. "They've got to pull through this in their own time; rest is what they need more than anything."

Joni wiped her sleeve over her face. "I know," she said. "Ignore me. It's just that I've never had to deal with anything like this before."

"Why don't you go home? You could take a bath and get something to eat," Amy suggested. "We have a lot of work ahead of us with these horses."

Joni nodded. "Thanks, Amy," she said, wiping her hands on her pants and doing a quick survey of the yard. "I'll see you in the morning then, if you're sure there's nothing else for me to do."

"Not a thing!" Amy flapped her hands at her and waved goodbye as Joni headed up the drive to her new car. Amy watched as the tail lights disappeared from sight. As she turned away, her gaze fell on the shadowy figure of the dead palomino and she was suddenly hit with a wave of nausea.

Needing to be alone for a few moments, Amy made her way to the barn and into the yearling's stall. To her astonishment, the colt whinnied and pricked his ears the moment he saw her. He crossed the stall on long, spindly legs as she closed the door behind her.

Amy very gently slid her arms around the yearling's neck, comforted beyond measure by his generous welcome. "Spindleberry," she murmured into the colt's mane. She knew she shouldn't be naming any of the horses from the trailer, but it suited the long-legged yearling perfectly.

The colt stood quietly while Amy closed her eyes. Her head was pounding and her throat ached with all the tears she had held back. Her fingers wrapped unconsciously around the colt's mane, and as her mind echoed again and again with the thud of the bolt pistol, she let herself cry. She couldn't remember a worse day since her mom had died.

Chapter Eight

Amy had a restless night's sleep. In the end she got up even earlier than usual and quietly made her way down to the office. It was too early to disturb the horses, so she logged on to the Internet and began to research livestock transportation, printing various pages of information and finding a number of useful details before she realized that nearly an hour had passed. Switching the computer off, Amy hurried to change into her yard clothes.

The first thing she did was check on the auction house horses. Spindleberry had eaten all of his feed and, by the way he pushed at Amy's hand when she peered over his door, was clearly looking for more. "Be patient, greedy." Amy laughed as he scraped at the floor with one hoof. Next, she went to the grey mare, who was lying down. Amy was relieved to see that most of the mash in her manger had been eaten.

"Morning, beautiful," she said, crouching down beside her. The grey mare sighed heavily. "I know, you probably don't feel very beautiful right now," Amy said, smoothing her neck. "But I promise, it won't be long before you feel better. I bet that by tomorrow you'll be on your feet, looking over the door for your breakfast." The mare gave a small snort and nosed at the straw, making it look as if she were contemplating the possibility. Amy smiled and rubbed the grey between the eyes before rising to her feet.

Next door, the chestnut gelding was also lying down, but he scrambled to his feet when Amy came into the stall. "Hello," she said softly, holding her hand out for the gelding to sniff. "Good boy," she whispered as he grazed his tongue over her hand. "You're looking much better!" She felt a surge of relief and reached her hand around the gelding's neck to give him a scratch behind the ears. The chestnut rested his nose on her head.

"Good boy," Amy murmured again before moving on to the old black gelding and bay mare. They both had a little less than half their feed left but had drunk their water. Their eyes looked too large in their faces, and Amy was sure that they were still in shock. She felt a rush of sympathy as she looked at their matted coats, and she decided to try to untangle their manes. Both horses had burrs knotted in their tails, and it was clear that they had been severely neglected in their previous home. Amy glanced at her watch and worked out that she had just under half an hour before it was time to start preparing the morning feeds. She grabbed a grooming kit from the tack room and spent a little time gently combing both horses' manes and gently currying their coats. She finished by massaging lavender oil into their skin. Remembering that Scott had been concerned about their heart rates, she decided to add some Hawthorn Berry to their feeds.

She was carefully measuring the doses of thick brown liquid when Joni arrived.

"What's that for?"

Amy thought the blonde stable hand was looking more like her usual self, although her eyes were still puffy.

"It's a heart tonic for the black and the bay," Amy explained, straightening up. "We could all use a little."

Joni flashed Amy a quick smile. "Do you want me to take over so you can get ready for school?" she offered.

"Well, I was about to start the rest of the feeds."

"I can do that. If you go and get changed now, you'll have time to help me turn the horses out." Joni held her hand out for the feed scoop.

Amy was extremely tempted at the thought of seeing Spindleberry's reaction to being outside after his terrible journey. "I would love to see Spindle explore the paddock now that he's feeling better," she admitted.

Joni raised her eyebrows. "Spindle?"

"Spindleberry – the yearling," Amy said, changing the subject quickly before Joni could ask why she had given one of the horses from the truck a name. "Well, you've persuaded me," she went on, handing over the feed scoop. "I think it's safe to give the three younger horses half a scoop of coarse mix with their mash, since they ate most of their supper last night. The mix should be easy enough to digest."

She left Joni in the feed room and jogged across the yard, kicking her boots off inside the kitchen door. "I'm going back out again in a minute," she told Lou before her sister had a chance to tell her to put her boots away properly. Amy thought she'd skip breakfast to save time, but suddenly her stomach gave a tremendous rumble.

"Have you eaten?" asked Lou.

Amy grinned. "It slipped my mind."

Lou shook her head, smiling. "I'll defrost you a couple of muffins while you're getting ready," she said.

"Where would I be without you?" Amy teased before heading upstairs.

As she began to wash, Amy's last words echoed in her head. Pretty soon she would have to do without Lou, once her sister was married to Scott. Amy shook her head to chase the thought away. She had more than enough to worry about just now.

The phone rang, and Lou shouted up to Amy that Ty wanted to speak with her. Amy ran down the stairs two at a time and was somewhat breathless as she reached for the handset.

"Hello?"

"Hi," said Ty. "I just wanted to let you know that Dad and I are headed to his office now. I should be back in a couple of hours, so will Joni be OK until then?"

"Sure," Amy told him. "I hope everything goes well."

"Fingers crossed," said Ty.

Amy remembered her Internet research and hurriedly filled Ty in on what she had discovered. "Scott was right, it is definitely illegal to use double-decker trailers to carry horses in Pennsylvania. Pretty soon, that'll be a nationwide law. But even in states where it's not illegal, if they have a law against the inhumane transport of horses or animals, that law can be used to prosecute people who transport horses in double-deckers. All you need is evidence that the trailer is cruel and unsuitable – and we have more than enough to prove that."

"That's good news, Amy," Ty said. "Thanks. We need all the help we can get."

"Good luck. I'll see you when I get back from school," Amy promised before she hung up.

Lou handed her the muffins, and Amy sat down at the table.

Lou asked her some questions about the research she'd done, and Amy filled her in on all the gruesome details, like the fact that double-deckers are often called torture trailers by animal rights groups and how a horse's organs systematically shut down in progressive stages of dehydration. Somehow, the new information made Amy less bewildered. She felt like they had a valid argument that the auction house's neglect was indeed criminal.

And while Amy believed their chances were better against the auction house, she knew how much Mr Baldwin had risked. He had disregarded his schedule and purposefully withheld information from his bosses until he was certain of the client's guilt. He made the right decisions for the horses, but they might not have been the best choices for his career – especially when his company had just laid off half its workforce. Amy hoped Mr Baldwin would be able to hold his ground and convince his bosses that he had the company's best interests in mind; but he would have a lot of explaining to do in what Amy guessed would be a short amount of time.

She didn't even want to think what would happen if Brad Baldwin lost his job. He'd probably blame Heartland, just as he had for Ty's accident. And no doubt he'd put the pressure back on Ty to find a job with a heftier pay cheque. Amy knew how hard it would be for Brad to locate another job if this company tarnished his reputation. The town wasn't very big, after all.

Amy pushed those thoughts from her mind. Nothing had been determined yet. Brad and Ty still had a chance. She finished her last mouthful and pushed her chair away from the table. "Thanks for the muffins, Lou. I'd better get going – I promised to help Joni turn the horses out."

Lou wiped her hands on a towel. "No problem. I'll probably head out soon and see if Joni needs a hand with anything. There's not much paperwork to do this morning."

"I'll tell her, I'm sure she'll be pleased." As Amy pulled open the kitchen door, she almost collided with Nancy, who was bursting in with her usual packed basket.

"Well!" Nancy exclaimed. "It seems the moment I'm not around to keep an eye on things, you have non-stop high drama!" The moment the words were out of her mouth she glanced at Lou, and it was clear she was wondering if she'd accidentally overstepped her bounds, implying that she was needed to keep order at Heartland.

But Lou smiled. "It wasn't a day any of us would like to repeat," she said.

Nancy turned back to Amy, placing her hand on her arm. "How are you, sweetheart? You don't look as if you managed to get much sleep last night."

"I didn't," Amy admitted. "But I'll be OK."

"Jack phoned and told me all about it," Nancy said. "How awful for you all. And those poor horses!"

"They're much better today. I was just about to turn them out in the paddock," Amy told her. "Do you want to come and see them?"

"I'd really like that," Nancy replied, looking pleased.

They made their way across the yard and into the barn, passing Joni, who was leading the chestnut mare down to the paddock.

"Don't worry," Joni smiled. "I left Spindleberry for you."

"Spindleberry. What a lovely name!" Nancy exclaimed.

"Well, it suits him," Amy said, feeling a rush of pride as she looked over the stall door at the colt. He nickered gently and then gave a snort when he noticed Amy was not alone.

She slid back the bolt. "Come on," she said, patting the yearling's neck and slipping on his halter. "It's time for you to stretch your legs."

"Yes, indeed," Nancy confirmed. "Spindleberry suits him fine."

Amy and Nancy walked on either side of the colt until they reached the paddock. Joni was on her way out and held open the gate for Amy to lead Spindleberry in. The yearling looked round and gave a long, loud snort. Amy slipped the halter off his head, then stepped back as the colt wheeled round and cantered to the far corner of the paddock, his black tail high. Amy thought that Spindleberry looked right at home.

It didn't take long for Amy to realize that Soraya was avoiding her in school. She didn't see her on the bus, and Soraya wasn't waiting for her in the hall before homeroom. Amy didn't feel like prolonging their petty disagreement, so she waited for Soraya at their usual table at lunchtime, hoping to patch things up. But when Soraya walked into the cafeteria, she took Amy aback by saying, "I'm sorry, but I can't sit with you today."

Amy tried to disguise her surprise as Soraya blurted out some excuse about having to discuss a history assignment with someone from her class. She barely made eye contact with Amy but fiddled with the fork on her tray until it fell off and clattered on to the floor. Amy bent down to pick it up and handed it back, but Soraya barely muttered her thanks.

Matt, who was standing just behind Soraya, cleared his throat and said, "I'll keep Amy company then, if you're going to be busy planning your assignment."

"I could really use your advice, too," Soraya said shortly.

Matt raised his eyebrows but said nothing. As Soraya walked away, Amy gave Matt a look of exasperation and muttered under her breath, "Don't ask."

He smiled awkwardly. "I'd better go with her. I'll catch you later, OK?" He gave her a small wave and followed Soraya across the cafeteria. Amy dropped her head in her hands. She could feel a headache coming on. *Soraya really knows how to pick her timing*, she thought. She knew that she could have tried to make up with her friend and maybe apologize for not being sympathetic enough, but she just didn't have the energy. Compared with what she had seen yesterday, her argument with Soraya seemed unimportant. Her thoughts quickly slipped to Ty and Brad. She wondered if their meeting with the trucking company was over and if they were happy with the outcome.

* * *

Amy found it impossible to concentrate as the afternoon dragged by endlessly. She lost count of the times she glanced at her watch until the school bus finally dropped her off and she was walking up the drive alongside the fields of horses.

Amy scanned the yard but didn't see Ty's truck. She shuddered at the thought of him and his dad still at the trucking office. She headed across to the top paddock to see the yearling before going in to get changed. She was surprised and delighted by the change in the horses just since the morning. They were all grazing, swishing their tails at flies, and looking as relaxed as any of the Heartland residents.

Amy dropped her bag on the ground and climbed on to the gate. "Spindle!" she called out. All of the horses threw up their heads to look in her direction.

"Spindleberry!" Amy called again. The yearling stared at her for a long moment and then broke into a canter. A few yards short of Amy, the colt pulled up short and tossed his head.

"Well, you've perked up," Amy remarked.

She slipped off the gate and began to walk over to the colt, but the yearling wheeled round and skittered away. It was obvious that he was less accustomed to being handled than he had appeared the day before. The shock and exhaustion must have made him more docile, Amy realized. The colt skidded to a halt and looked back at her, but Amy decided not to push her luck. She would get changed and come back out to spend some proper time with the horses.

She climbed over the gate, and when she bent to pick up her bag she became aware of four long legs on the other side of the fence. "Hello, cheeky." Amy straightened up and laughed at Spindleberry's pricked ears and alert expression.

"I'll come back soon," she promised, slowly stretching out her hand. Spindleberry snorted, but he allowed Amy to stroke his neck and pull a prickly burr from his mane before she headed up to the farmhouse.

Amy felt her stomach lurch as she approached the backside of the trailer, expecting to see the evidence of yesterday's trauma. A wave of relief washed over her when she realized that the horses' bodies must have been picked up when she was at school. Amy waved to Joni, who was sweeping the far end of the yard, before pushing open the door to the kitchen.

Ty was sitting at the table with Lou and Jack. They all looked up as Amy walked in.

"Ty! You're here!" Amy exclaimed. "But I didn't see your truck."

"Dad dropped me off about half an hour ago."

"Well, how did it go?" Amy asked at once, dumping her bag on the floor.

"Thank goodness you're back so we can all find out," said Lou. "Ty refused to tell us anything until you came home!"

Amy took a chair opposite Ty and looked expectantly at him. He was still in his nice clothes – a button-down shirt and khakis.

"Maybe a cup of coffee would be nice before I begin?" he suggested. "Or we could have a bite to eat first?" He kept his face poker straight, but Amy knew when he was teasing.

"Ty!" she scolded. "Come on, we're waiting."

He held up his hands, laughing. "OK, OK. I'll tell you." He became more serious, but his good mood was still obvious. "It went well for Dad. He's not going to lose his job," he announced.

"That's great!" Amy and Lou spoke at the same time.

"There's more." Ty smiled. "Dad had decided to report the auction house to the authorities even before the meeting, but when we showed his boss all of the evidence, he promised to support Dad all the way. He said he would terminate the contract with the auction house, but he asked Dad to take care of the legal responsibilities. So Dad has to meet with the police and make a formal statement."

"That's such good news!" Amy was so thrilled that she jumped up and gave Ty an enthusiastic hug. "I can't believe how much your dad has done for those horses! I'm so glad the new bosses listened and everything. I've been worried about it all day," she confessed.

Jack pushed his chair back and declared, "This calls for a celebration!" He crossed over to the fridge and opened the door.

"Hang on," Ty said quickly. "It's not all good news, I'm afraid."

Jack slowly closed the door and frowned. "What do you mean?"

"Dad's company only has so much power," Ty explained. "They can refuse to take the horses to Georgia, but the auction house still owns the horses." He paused before saying quietly, "They demanded that we release them as soon as possible."

"No!" Amy exclaimed in horror. "They can't have them back, not after the way they've treated them."

"But they're the legal owners," Ty told her, his voice sounding weak.

"I won't let them go back," Amy insisted. "What about your dad going to the police?"

"He's filed the papers, but the auction house can continue business during the investigation," Ty explained. "They're sending a couple of employees down in a few days to get the horses," he went on resignedly. "And the trailer as well."

"I can't believe this!" Amy stood up and began to pace. "What's the point of keeping the horses here until then? We're just plumping them up so there'll be more meat on them for the slaughter." Then she was struck by a horrifying thought. "They're not planning on driving them away in that death trap, are they?"

"I don't know," Ty said helplessly.

Amy stared at him for a moment. "But there's nothing we can do to stop them. It might be illegal in Pennsylvania, but if it's not illegal in Virginia..." Her voice trailed away, and she struggled not to panic. She had to keep her head clear and try to figure out if there was any way she could possibly prevent the auction house from getting the horses back.

"Sit down, Amy," Lou said with concern. "I'm sure we can find a way to stop them from taking the horses if we think hard enough."

"I can't think about it now," Amy said automatically. "I need some fresh air. I'll be back in a few minutes."

"Take your time." As usual, Grandpa seemed to sense that she needed to be outside with the horses, where she could always think more clearly.

Amy headed straight to the paddock. She climbed over the gate and walked over to Spindleberry, who was quietly grazing under a tree. The yearling flicked his ears towards her as she approached, but he didn't move away. *It's amazing how horses seem to know when people need them*, Amy thought. She sat down in the grass and leaned against the tree.

She looked at Spindleberry's large brown eyes. They were widely spaced, suggesting an honest temperament and a willingness to learn. He was just beginning to trust her, so how could she let someone take him away? "Oh, Spindle," she sighed. "I just don't know what to do to save you." The colt lifted his head when he heard his name, and Amy's heart filled with helplessness.

Chapter Nine

Joni gave Duke a healthy pat as she tethered him to a ring in the aisle. Amy was so wrapped up in her own troubles that it took her a moment to realize that Joni was looking at Duke with a worried expression.

"Is everything all right?" she asked, walking over to the dark bay horse.

Joni hesitated. "I didn't want to bother you, with everything else that's going on."

Amy's heart sank. She didn't know if she could cope with hearing any more bad news. "What's wrong?"

"It's Duke," Joni told her. "I'm having trouble getting him to go into the barn. The grey from the auction house is in his stall for now, so I put him in a smaller stall last night. Although he seemed a bit unnerved by it, he eventually settled down. But when I tried to lead him in tonight, he absolutely refused. He got himself into quite a state, blowing hard and sweating."

Joni had Amy's immediate attention. Amy and Lou had arranged to buy Duke from Green Briar after he had been badly treated there. The last thing she wanted now was for him to suffer a setback, not when he was so close to being ready to be rehomed.

"Do you think he's upset by being in a different stall?" Amy suggested.

Joni looked thoughtful. "I'm sure that's got something to do with it, but to be honest, his reaction is so drastic, I wonder if there could be something more."

At that moment, the farmhouse door banged open and Ty walked out.

"Is everything OK?" he asked when he reached them. Amy repeated what Joni had told her.

Ty patted Duke, who was resting one of his hind legs and looking unconcerned as he dozed in the late afternoon sunshine. "The best thing would be for us to watch you lead him. Maybe we can tell what triggers it."

"Sure." Joni untied Duke and clicked softly to him. Duke walked obediently after her until they reached the entrance to the barn. As soon as Joni tried to get him to follow her inside, Duke dug in his hooves and laid his ears back. His whole body strained against her when Joni gave a firm tug on the lead line.

"Hang on," Ty called. "Let me turn on the light for you." He disappeared into the barn, and Amy heard him flick the switch a couple of times. "The bulb must have burned out," Ty said, reappearing. "Duke's probably anxious about going into dark, confined spaces after what happened with the tornado." Amy nodded in agreement, recalling that Duke had been one of the horses trapped in the barn when it collapsed.

Joni looked frustrated with herself. "I should have thought of that."

"Not at all," Amy assured her. "You couldn't have known Duke's full history. But I think Ty's right. Duke's probably suffering from an equine version of claustrophobia. We need to fix the light and maybe give the grey mare the smaller stall that Duke was in."

She went into the feed room and picked up a bottle of Rescue Remedy. Back outside, she poured a few drops on to her hand and encouraged Duke to lick it. "Good boy," she murmured.

She began to work small T-touch circles over him while Joni held the lead rope and smoothed his velvety chestnut muzzle. They could hear the clanging of a stepladder as Ty changed the bulb inside the barn. After a while, Duke gave a deep sigh and Amy felt the tension start to leave him.

Ty walked out of the barn, brushing his hands on his jeans. "The light's fixed," he told them. "Why don't you try taking him in again, Joni? The end stall is empty and it's got an extra window, so I think it'd be good for Duke."

Amy stood back to give them space. Joni took a few steps and then gently coaxed Duke to follow her into the doorway. Duke let out a loud snort when he was halfway through, and Joni immediately stopped and gave him time to make sure that he was safe. She spoke in soft tones, reassuring him until he had followed her down to the end stall.

"That's terrific," said Joni, looking pleased as she shut the door. "I can't believe the difference. He's like another horse, just because of the light."

Duke began pulling contentedly at a haynet, one eye on the people watching him over the half-door.

"You know, it was good that you could tell Duke was genuinely scared of going into his stall," said Ty.

Joni raised her eyebrows. "What do you mean?"

"Lots of people would have assumed that he was just being difficult and wouldn't have tried to figure out why he was acting up," Ty told her. "They might have tried to force him into the stall, and that would have been a big setback in terms of his recovery."

Joni smiled. "My mom once told me that it's very rare for a horse to act up just for the sake of it. She believes that there's nearly always a reason for a horse refusing to obey you."

Amy stared at Joni. "Of course," she breathed. "That must be it." She didn't know why she hadn't thought of it before.

"What?" Ty asked.

Amy looked at them both. "Thanks to Duke, I think I know what's wrong with Apollo!"

Amy dialled Ben's number, and the first thing she did when he answered was apologize for not having been in touch sooner. "We've had a bit of a crisis here," she told him, before explaining what had happened over the weekend.

"It was awful," she admitted. "But the worst part is still to come. The auction house has demanded that we return the survivors. And legally, it's their right to claim the horses they almost killed."

"That's insane," Ben said under his breath. "Isn't there anything you can do to stop them?"

Amy sighed. "Believe me, I've thought about making a midnight run with the horses in tow. Taking them somewhere they can't be found or hurt. But then I get a dose of reality."

"Which is?"

"That I'd be breaking the law. And that wouldn't look good for Heartland. Besides, the horses aren't in any shape for a long trek. They need their rest."

"Look, you've done everything you can," Ben told her. "The point is all those horses might have died if Brad hadn't brought them to Heartland. You saved them, Amy."

"Yes, but what have we saved them for?" Amy asked unhappily. "More torture?"

There was a long pause before Ben changed the subject. "Have you had any thoughts on Apollo? I understand if you haven't, you've had more than enough on your mind..."

"That's actually why I was calling," Amy said, relieved to be discussing a horse that she could definitely help. Or at least she hoped she could. "Something happened with Duke tonight that gave me an idea about Apollo."

"Go on," Ben prompted.

"Duke wouldn't walk into the barn. His reaction reminded me a little of Apollo's — you know, resisting as if he were just being disobedient but looking really scared. We figured out that the light was burned out in the barn, and we had moved him into a smaller stall. He seemed to suffer from some kind of claustrophobia."

"That seems plausible," Ben commented, "considering he was inside the barn the night of the tornado. But what's that got to do with Apollo? He doesn't mind going in the barn. He really likes the barn."

"Exactly," Amy agreed. "Duke made me wonder if Apollo

might have the same problem, only reversed."

"Agoraphobia, you mean?"

"Exactly." Amy crossed the room to look out the window. "Maybe Apollo had a bad experience outside that gave him a fear of wide-open spaces."

"That's an idea," Ben said. "Can you hang on a second while I get Tara? You can explain it to her and see what she thinks."

"Oh, is she there?"

"Yes, she came over to watch a DVD about the US show-jumping team."

While Amy waited, she watched Joni and Ty leading the rest of the horses from the field for the night. The grey and the chestnut mare walked quietly beside them, and Amy felt a pang of emotion. She was thrilled by the way the animals were recovering, even though they still showed all the hallmarks of neglect, with dull coats and gaunt ribs. But she was also incredibly sad that they couldn't stay at Heartland and be cared for until they became healthy, well-adjusted animals, ready for rehoming.

Amy's thoughts were interrupted when Tara came to the phone. "Hi, Amy. Ben said you have some news for me."

"I hope so." Amy smiled into the handset. "I think that I've figured out what might be upsetting Apollo, but I need to ask you something first."

"Shoot."

"Has Apollo ever had a traumatic experience when he was outside? Maybe he was scared in a pasture or some other open space?"

"How do you know that?" Tara sounded surprised. "Yes, there was a time when he had a real scare. It was the first time that he bolted with me."

"What happened?" Amy asked, even more convinced now that she was on the right track.

"It was at our first show together," said Tara. "He was pretty wound up, so I took him away from the rings to a quieter section of the show ground to warm him up." Amy listened intently, picturing the scene. She would have done exactly the same thing with an inexperienced horse. "I was so wrapped up in working Apollo that I wasn't really sure what happened until later," Tara went on. "There was a huge noise above me, and then Apollo reared in the air, spun round, and galloped off. He swerved to avoid someone, and I fell off."

"Were you OK?" Amy asked.

Tara laughed. "Yes, I was fine. My pride took a beating, though. Apollo showed up at our trailer a few minutes later without a scratch, thank goodness."

Amy felt herself warming to Tara more and more. "So what was the noise?"

"It turned out that one of the riders competing had taken a bad fall, and a helicopter was called to airlift her to the hospital. The helicopter landed just behind us. Even though I heard it, I didn't actually see anything."

"But Apollo probably could see it, because horses have a much wider range of vision," Amy finished for her.

"Exactly," Tara replied. "He must have thought a monstrous

bird was coming down to get him." She paused and then asked, "Does that help with your diagnosis?"

"It does," Amy assured her. "It explains a lot. I'm almost certain that Apollo is agoraphobic. He's fine working in enclosed spaces where he feels secure, but the moment you ask him to go out into an open space, I think he gets nervous and suffers something similar to a panic attack."

"You mean, he thinks that he might be attacked by something flying out of the sky again?"

"Yes," Amy replied.

"But that doesn't make sense at all! I mean, that all happened ages ago. It's been four years, and he's been fine since then, and he's fine grazing in the paddock. He only started spooking and bolting since we moved to Nick's yard."

Amy thought it through. "What were the grounds like at your other stable? Didn't you say that the trainer didn't allow you to ride out on the trails?" she pointed out.

"Yes, that's true," Tara said slowly. "And the paths between the barn and the outdoor rings were fenced on both sides."

"Well, maybe he hasn't felt as exposed since the helicopter incident. I think there's something about Nick's set-up that reminds Apollo of it," Amy said hesitantly. "And I think that he might have lost his faith in you when it comes to riding outside the ring."

"Really? What do you mean?" Tara sounded startled.

"Well, it wasn't your fault at all, and there was no way you could help it, but you fell off," Amy explained, hoping Tara wouldn't take offence. "In his eyes, especially since he was a young horse, he might have felt that you were abandoning him."

"You really think so?" Tara questioned solemnly. "That sounds serious."

"We can work through it," Amy reassured her. "I think it's going to be best if I come over there. We need Apollo to start feeling safe when he's ridden in the fields and on the trails near his home yard. If I show you some techniques to gain Apollo's trust, you'll be able to help him overcome his fear on your own."

"That's incredible," said Tara. "I never would have thought it could stem all the way back to that show. Ben said that you'd be able to help, but to be honest, I had my doubts. I was sure that if I couldn't work it out with my own horse, then no one else would be able to."

"I'll see if I can get Ty to drive me over tomorrow, right after school," Amy promised.

"Thanks, Amy. I'll look forward to seeing you then." Tara sounded hopeful, and as Amy hung up she smiled at how good it was to have something positive to think about.

She went out into the yard and met Ty coming back up from the paddock, looking frustrated. "I swear that bay colt is getting worse," he said when he saw her.

Amy's heart skipped a beat. "Worse? What do you mean? He was fine earlier."

"He's so full of himself," Ty explained, wiping his forehead. "He won't let me near him."

Amy felt her shoulders sag with relief. "It does seem like he's getting more boisterous as he becomes more comfortable here," she agreed. "I'm starting to wonder if he's ever really been properly handled."

Ty frowned. "Do you think he was just left in a field until he was old enough to be sold to the auction house?"

Amy nodded. "It's a possibility, don't you think?"

"I guess so."

Amy reached out for the halter and rope. "Do you want me to try?"

"Sure." Ty passed them to her and walked with her back down to the paddock. As they went, Amy told Ty about her conversation with Ben and Tara.

"That's great." Ty sounded pleased. "I can pick you up and take you over to Nick's after school."

"Thanks," Amy said. She glanced sideways at Ty and grinned, already looking forward to spending a little time with him on her own, away from all their present worries.

Spindleberry was contentedly cropping the grass and didn't even look up when they climbed the fence and started to walk across the field. Amy hid the halter and lead rope behind her back. Spindleberry allowed her to get within reach of him.

"Hey there, boy," Amy said gently.

Spindleberry raised his head and stared at her, his nostrils flaring. Then to Amy's surprise, he took a step towards her. She stroked his neck before slipping the halter over his head. She led the yearling to the gate, which Ty had already opened. "I guess it's just that I've spent the most time with him," Amy said apologetically.

"It's more than that. I think he's really bonded with you," Ty told her. "After all, you were the one who treated him when he first came off the trailer."

Amy scratched Spindleberry behind the ears and smiled as the colt lipped at her sleeve. "I think he's terrific," she admitted.

"You always like the stubborn ones," Ty added, rolling his eyes.

As they began to walk towards the barn, Ty seemed to be deep in thought. They led Spindleberry into his stall, and Amy slid the bolt closed on the door.

"Amy..." Ty hesitated. "I'm sure you know this, but it's important that you don't get too close to any of these horses. I'm afraid of how hard it's going to be when they leave."

Amy saw the concern in Ty's eyes and reached out to touch his arm. "Thanks for caring so much," she said softly. She looked into the stall where Spindleberry was attacking the feed in his bucket by shaking his head from side to side. "I guess I've just got this tiny hope deep down inside that the auction house is bluffing. That they'll take the chance to get rid of these horses and just leave them with us..." Her voice trailed away as Ty began to shake his head.

"I'm sorry, Amy. They called earlier when you were down in the paddock. I came out to find you, but then I got distracted by the problem with Duke."

Amy's stomach lurched. "What did they say?"

Ty looked as if he could hardly bring himself to say the words. "They're coming on Wednesday," he said at last.

"Oh, Ty," Amy whispered. "What are we going to do now?"

Chapter Ten

Ty was waiting for Amy outside school the next day. "Hey, how are you?" he asked as she climbed in beside him.

"OK, I guess. But the whole day was a blur. How am I supposed to concentrate on the Versailles Treaty with everything that's going on around here?" Amy questioned.

"I'm afraid I can't help you there," Ty said with a comforting smile as he started the engine, checked his mirrors, and pulled off.

"It doesn't help that Soraya is avoiding me," Amy confessed. "Every time I see her, she's rushing off to do something else. It's just stupid that we can't talk it over and make up. It'd be really nice to have her support right now."

Ty's voice sounded apologetic. "I know I'm a poor substitute, but if you're desperate, you can always talk to me."

Amy laughed. "You're the first person I turn to, you know that." She glanced at his profile and felt a tug of emotion. She couldn't put into words just how much Ty's support meant to her. She didn't know where she would be without him.

"So," Ty went on, "do you want to tell me what happened with Soraya?"

Amy suddenly realized that she hadn't confided in anyone about her quarrel with Soraya. Everyone had been so focused on the auction horses over the last couple of days, it hadn't come up. "Do you mind if we talk about it after we've been to see Apollo?" she asked. "I'd really like to hear your thoughts on him before we get there."

Ty nodded and Amy described how she thought it was best to build up trust between Tara and Apollo. "Maybe she could help you when you're doing the join-up?" he suggested. "That way Apollo would build his connection with her more than you."

Amy agreed and then leaned her head against the window and looked out at the traffic in the other lane. She was looking forward to introducing Ty to Tara. Amy hoped he would like her as much as she did, since it was looking like Tara and Ben might become a couple.

When they pulled up at the yard, Ben and Tara were waiting for them. "Thanks so much for this," Tara said as soon as Amy and Ty joined them.

"We're just happy to help," Amy smiled. She walked across the yard with Tara, with Ben and Ty following behind. At one point, Amy heard Ben ask about the auction horses. She didn't catch Ty's low response but guessed that he had told Ben that the horses were being picked up the next day. She pushed the thought to the back of her mind and made herself concentrate on Apollo.

At the sound of their footsteps in the barn, Apollo stuck his head over the stall door and nickered softly. Tara's face broke into a broad smile. "It's such a shame that I haven't been able to ride him out on the trails," she told Amy. "He's a perfect horse in every other way. I know that he'd love the trails!"

Amy nodded in agreement. "All we have to do now is

convince him." She turned to Ty. "What do you think?"

Ty ran his eye critically over Apollo and studied his beautiful white head. "The same as you," he said at last. "You can tell that he's an honest horse. He doesn't look like the type to act out of malice."

Tara's eyes widened. "How can you tell that just by looking at him?"

"By looking at his features," Ty replied. "The size and shape of the ears, eyes and nostrils, and the lines of the mouth and chin can give you a really good understanding of a horse's nature. You can also look at the hairs on the horse's face. See how Apollo has a swirl right here?" He traced the hairs on Apollo's forehead. "If a horse has one swirl in the middle of the forehead, then you can generally assume that he will have a trustworthy nature."

"Wow!" Tara glanced at Ben with her eyebrows raised.

"What did I tell you?" Ben grinned, and Amy felt a rush of delight that Ben obviously believed in the work they did.

They led Apollo down to the ring, and Amy explained that she wanted Tara to shadow her movements as she tried to join up with him. "Apollo is relaxed working in the ring, so that's one obstacle we don't have," she said. "All you need to do is to stand very close to me and do exactly what I do."

"OK," said Tara, sounding a little nervous.

"You'll be fine," Amy reassured her. "I'll talk you through everything."

They stood in the centre of the ring, and Amy told Tara to send Apollo out to the side. Tara nodded and flicked the longline at Apollo's quarters. Apollo snorted in surprise but moved away from Tara. She flicked the line again, and he cantered away to the fence, his ears flattened.

After the gelding had cantered six circuits, Amy said to Tara, "Get ready. We're going to get him to turn around." She stepped towards Apollo to block his action, and he recognized the obstacle and whirled round in the opposite direction. Tara kept exactly in time, following Amy's every move.

"Can you see his ear?" Amy asked.

"The way it's pointing inward?" Tara asked.

"Yes. That means he's ready to join up with us," Amy explained.

"What happens next?" Tara couldn't keep the excitement out of her voice.

Amy watched the beautiful grey horse canter round the ring, his stride strong and fluid. After a few more strides, he lowered his head and dropped into an effortless, floating trot.

"What does that mean?" Tara questioned as Apollo stretched down his neck and began to lick and chew with his mouth.

"It means we're almost there. Now we turn so our shoulders are pointed at him, and we drop our eye contact," Amy said. She could just see Apollo out of the corner of her eye. He had slowed to a stop and was looking over in their direction. "He'll walk up to us now. When he does, turn and rub him gently between the eyes before turning your back again," Amy told Tara. She waited until she heard Apollo approach and Tara make a quiet fuss over him. Then Amy murmured, "You've got to show him that you're no threat to him whatsoever. Move away from him with me, and he will probably follow." She stepped forward and heard Tara's exclamation of delight as Apollo walked after them.

Wherever they went, Apollo followed until it was clear they had earned his full trust. Then they both turned and quietly rewarded Apollo by patting him.

"That was incredible!" Tara exclaimed, her eyes shining.

Amy smiled, totally understanding what Tara was feeling. "By doing join-up, you're using a horse's instinct as a herd animal to help build a unique bond of trust."

"And you think it was broken when I fell off at the show ground?" said Tara.

Amy hesitated. "It's clear from how he responds to you both in the stable and in the ring that he still trusts you. I think that it's more a case that he's lost his faith in you when it comes to open spaces, especially when it's an unfamiliar place. He thinks that if he's attacked, he's going to be left on his own. So the next step is for you to try to join up away from the ring."

"When do you think he'll be ready for that?" Tara asked.

"Now's as good a time as any," Amy declared. "Let's let him rest a few minutes and give it a try."

As they walked Apollo round the ring, Ben paused. "What would you think about me getting Red, and we could ride alongside Apollo? It might help him settle down if he's got another horse with him. Kind of like he would follow the lead horse in the wild."

"Good idea." Amy and Ty endorsed Ben's suggestion

simultaneously and then smiled at each other.

It only took Ben five minutes to tack up Red and ride over to join them. The chestnut gelding's coat was gleaming. "He looks fantastic, Ben," Amy said admiringly.

"He's certainly settled in well," Ben agreed as he nudged Red in front of Apollo.

As soon as they walked Apollo on the path that led to the outside gate, he put his ears flat against his head and his hooves solid on the ground. When he wouldn't move forward, Amy started to massage him with circular movements along his neck.

"What will that do?" asked Tara.

"It's to help him relax," Amy replied, working her fingers until she felt the tension begin to leave the gelding. "Now then, boy, just one step at a time," she murmured. Amy looked at Tara. "Keep him close to the fence at first so he feels more secure," she suggested.

"OK." Tara clicked to Apollo, who hesitated once more before stepping forward through the gate. He let out a loud snort but walked beside Tara along the stretch of the fence.

Amy handed Tara the lunge line. "Just do exactly what we did before. Keep him on the lunge line this time, though. We don't want him bolting for home or taking off in the other direction." Tara nodded, her face set with determination.

Amy walked across the field to join Ty at the gate. "How do you think they'll do?"

"I'm optimistic," Ty replied, looking thoughtful. "He's a great horse who's eager to please, and it's obvious that Tara dotes on him. If that's not enough to get him over his fear, then I don't know what is."

Amy shaded her eyes from the sun. Ben had halted Red next to Apollo. Despite having the comfort of another horse near, the big grey gelding was standing with his muscles taut. Amy thought he looked as if he could explode at any moment. Chewing her bottom lip, Tara gave the signal for Apollo to walk on, and Ben nudged Red forward as well.

Apollo staggered with his first step, and Amy worried that he would panic and dash back to the gate. Instead, he found his pace behind Red and finished the circle. As Tara sent him forward into a canter, it was clear that Apollo was focusing on her instead of his fear.

"It's amazing the effect that just one join-up has had on him," Amy commented. Although the grey's stride wasn't as smooth as it had been in the training ring, the fact that he was willing to be worked in an open field was already a tremendous achievement.

Tara was clearly not only very competent but a fast learner, as she repeated everything they had done in the schooling ring. When Apollo was settled, Ben directed Red to the far side of the field so that Tara was working her horse alone.

"That's good," Ty commented as Tara began encouraging Apollo away from the fence. Little by little they edged away until they were almost in the middle of the field. By now, Apollo was showing all the signs of wanting to join up, so Tara dropped her aggressive stance and turned away from him.

Amy reached out and gripped Ty's arm. "This is it," she

whispered. "This is the point when he's going to feel alone. He'll either feel afraid and try to run, or he'll put his trust in Tara."

Apollo hesitated, staring at his owner in the centre of the field. Then he swung his quarters round and slowly walked to her. Amy felt a surge of happiness as Tara made a fuss over Apollo before walking away. Apollo moved forward at once, following wherever she went. When Tara stopped to praise her horse again, Ben gave her a celebratory thumbs-up sign.

"So, it's another happy ending," Ty said, sounding amused.

"You could say that!" Amy laughed.

Tara slid the bolt closed on Apollo's stall. "I still can't believe it," she said for the umpteenth time. "It was like waving a magic wand."

"It's not usually that easy," Amy admitted. "It often takes a lot of time and hard work to get that kind of result. You were lucky you already had such a strong bond with him."

"And don't forget that you're only part of the way there," Ty added. "You'll need to continue joining up with Apollo on a regular basis."

"Yes, and when you are ready to hit the trails, make sure that for the first few times, you go with other horses," Amy suggested.

"That won't be a problem. Red and I'd be happy to accompany them," said Ben with a little blush. "Tara could try some Bach Flower Remedies, too, couldn't she?"

"Definitely," Amy agreed. "The best one for Apollo would be

Star of Bethlehem — it's for delayed trauma, so it doesn't matter that Apollo's scare was a while ago. You can also give him Larch to increase his confidence and Mimulus to help him conquer his fear."

"That sounds interesting. I've never given him herbal remedies before," said Tara. "Is there anything else I should try?"

Amy thought. "You could put a jar of geranium-scented oil in his stall," she said. "It helps to eradicate fear."

"Fantastic!" Tara exclaimed in her usual enthusiastic way, and Amy didn't miss the fond glance that Ben gave her.

As they walked past Storm's stall, Amy couldn't resist looking in. "Sorry, Daniel's taken him to a show," Ben told her.

"Never mind, I can see him next time," she answered, trying not to feel disappointed. It was great to know that Storm was fulfilling his potential as a competition horse, but it was hard to forget that she had once shared the same bond with him as Tara had with Apollo.

When they reached the car, Ben and Tara thanked them again, and Ben said, "What do you think about the four of us going out sometime soon? Maybe we could go to a movie or bowling?"

"That sounds like fun." Amy smiled, thinking it would be nice to strike up a friendship with Tara.

"You could ask Soraya and Matt, too, and the six of us could go," Ben suggested.

Amy hesitated, not sure how Soraya would react to the idea. Before she could think of the right words, Ty rescued her. "That's a great idea. We'll get back to you on it once things have calmed down with the auction horses and everything."

Ben and Tara hadn't seemed to notice that there was anything wrong, and as they drove away, Amy said gratefully, "Thanks, Ty."

"No problem," he replied, reaching to turn down the radio. "Now do you want to talk about what's going on between you and Soraya?"

"We had a stupid fight on Saturday," Amy confessed. "It's just that lately all Soraya seems to do is complain about Ashley and Matt. She thinks that he cares about Ashley more than he should. Of course, I pointed out to her that Matt is a nice guy, and she should appreciate that. And she pointed out that I was taking sides." Amy struggled to be fair. "And while I feel like she worries about Matt too much, she probably feels the same about me and Heartland."

"Soraya has to understand that you've been kind of distracted with the auction horses," Ty said.

Amy hesitated, fiddling with a roll of twine on the dashboard. "I haven't really had a chance to tell her what's been going on," she admitted. "We haven't talked all week."

Ty went quiet for a while. "I've got a feeling that she'll be pretty upset when she finds out everything that's happened and that you haven't included her," he said at last. "She'd want to be there for you, Amy."

Amy felt frustrated. It was never easy being told you were in the wrong, no matter how gently. "As far as I'm concerned, I would have told her if she were capable of thinking of anything other than Matt," she insisted. "I really don't want to talk about it any more."

"That's fine," Ty replied. "But Soraya's feelings about Matt are real to her, and she confided in you because you're her best friend. Don't you think she'd expect you to do the same?"

Amy didn't reply. She leaned her head against the window and tried to push away the uncomfortable feeling that Ty was right. She didn't know how she'd let the disagreement with Soraya continue for so long.

Chapter Eleven

The next morning, Amy was up early and headed outside before Ty or Joni arrived. It was the last chance she would have to spend time on her own with the auction horses and, in particular, Spindleberry.

When she walked into the barn and flicked on the lights, Spindleberry's was one of the first heads to appear over a door. The colt greeted her with a friendly nicker, clearly anticipating his breakfast. Amy smiled sadly. He had only been with them a few days and already he had settled into the Heartland routine as if it were home to him. She smoothed his nose before going to mix the morning feeds. As she did, her thoughts stayed on the yearling. His behaviour indicated that he had had little contact with humans over the course of his short life. Amy was convinced that he had never been trained to be tied up or have his hooves picked, which were some of the basics taught to a foal.

An idea started to take hold in Amy's head. She thought that if she could get Spindleberry to stand quietly while being tied and obediently lift up his hooves, then he might be appealing to a buyer at the auction. Someone might want him as a riding horse. He could go for something other than… Amy shook her head, refusing to think of the alternative.

After finishing with the feeds, Amy went to Spindleberry's stall. He looked up expectantly. "You'll have your breakfast soon, I promise," she told him. "But first, I need you to be a good boy for me." Amy gently slipped a halter over the yearling's head. She led Spindleberry over to the ring set into the wall and looped the rope through the ring in a quick-release knot. Spindleberry sniffed curiously at the rope but stayed calm, and Amy realized how much the yearling was beginning to trust her. She stayed for a moment smoothing his neck before quietly moving away. Spindleberry tried to follow her. The moment he felt the restraint, he shook his head and jerked his body, trying desperately to free himself.

"Steady, Spindleberry, easy now," Amy said soothingly. Spindleberry's ear flickered in her direction, but he still continued to pull. "Easy," Amy called again and was pleased when the yearling stood still. Even though he was quiet, his body was tense all over. Amy let herself back into the stall and began to work T-touch over him, letting her fingers rub deep into his coat.

Gradually, Spindleberry relaxed and gave a long snort. "Good boy," Amy murmured. She gently untied him and slipped off the halter. Spindleberry gave his body a thorough shake, looking comical with his thin front legs splayed like a fawn's, supporting his quavering body. Amy gave him one final pat before going to distribute the feeds. Spindle's first lesson had gone well, but would it be worth anything in the end? A sickening mix of hope and fear churned in her stomach.

Once all of the horses were nose deep in their breakfasts, Amy suddenly felt hungry for her own. She made her way back to the house and was surprised to find Lou already up and making coffee. "You're awake early," Amy remarked.

"I couldn't sleep," Lou confessed. "I kept thinking all night that today's the day the horses are being taken away."

Amy nodded. "There's no way I'm going to school," she declared. "There's no point. I can't concentrate. I promise I'll catch up on everything I miss at the weekend, though."

Lou didn't try to convince Amy otherwise.

"I can't believe there's nothing we can do," Amy said in frustration. "And they're all doing so well now."

Her sister carried a pan of scrambled eggs across to the table. "Tell me about them," she prompted.

Amy helped herself to a piece of toast and held out her plate for the eggs. "Thanks," she said. "How did you know I was hungry?"

Lou grinned. "Sisterly intuition."

Amy swallowed a mouthful of buttery eggs. "The two older horses that Scott had to give IVs are still weak, but if they were given a decent period of time to put on some weight, they would be fine." She paused to take a sip of coffee. "The grey and the chestnut are younger, and although their condition was obviously bad even before they were loaded, they've both recovered surprisingly quickly. By the look of their stable manners, all four of them have been kept as riding horses at some point, which makes it even worse that this is how they've ended up. It's just so infuriating." Amy grew indignant, and she stabbed fiercely at the butter for her second piece of toast.

"What about the fifth horse, the yearling?" Lou asked.

Amy felt a warm glow inside her. "He's wonderful, Lou. He's got such a great personality, and he's a quick learner, too. He'd make a wonderful riding horse." Her voice trailed off, and she glanced up in time to see the sympathy in Lou's eyes.

"I'm so sorry, Amy," her sister said softly.

Amy couldn't bring herself to speak, and at that moment Jack came into the room. He joined them at the table. "Lou and I were up until late last night talking about the auction horses," he said, putting his hand over Amy's. "We spent hours going through the books, trying to find enough money to put in an offer for them."

Amy's heart leaped, but she knew deep down what her grandfather's next sentence would be. "I'm really sorry, but there is just no way we can raise that kind of sum," he said gently. "It would mean not having enough money to feed the horses we already have."

Amy forced a smile on to her face and said, "It's OK, Grandpa. I appreciate you trying. We've just got to hope that the horses are bought by decent people at the next auction." She knew as she was saying it that there was little hope that horses in their condition would go for anything other than meat, but there was no point making them all feel even more upset.

Jack squeezed her hand and stood up. "At least we can make that horrible trailer as comfortable as possible for their journey," he said. "I'd like to think they'd bring one that's more suitable, but I wouldn't count on it."

Amy nodded. "We can make sure that they're fed and

watered properly," she added. "And given a nice grooming."

It seemed like so little, but it was the only thing they could do for the horses now.

Right after breakfast, Lou went into her office and shut the door. Amy guessed it was so she wouldn't have to watch the departure of the auction horses. Before Amy went back out to the yard, the phone rang.

It was Ben. "Hi, Amy. I won't keep you. Tara and I just wanted you to know that we tried riding Red and Apollo in the field yesterday, and Apollo even did a short dressage session! He looked fantastic. We wanted to tell you that Heartland can claim another success story." He paused and his voice lowered. "So, is there any news on the auction horses?"

"No, they're still leaving us," Amy said flatly, listening to his exclamation of dismay.

Amy thanked Ben for phoning. *At least we've had one bit of good news today*, she thought as she hung up and walked towards the kitchen door. Joni and Ty were already hard at work mucking out when she reached the barn. Amy joined them, and they finished the stalls without any of the usual jokes and chatter.

When all of the chores were finished and Ty and Joni were leading the Heartland horses down to the fields, Amy went back to the barn to check on Spindleberry. He nuzzled at her hands as she gave him an alfalfa cube. She was determined to spoil him for the last few hours he was there. "Now then," she told him, "I'm going to introduce you to the joys of grooming."

Spindleberry blinked his long-lashed eyes at her as if he understood exactly what she was saying.

"A brisk brush first, to get all the muck out of your coat," she said, showing him the brush and allowing him to sniff it. Spindleberry pulled back in surprise as his velvety nose made contact with the stiff bristles. Amy laughed before gently placing it on his neck and drawing it over his coat. She told herself that what she was doing was worth it, if only for Spindleberry's enjoyment. The colt swung his head round to watch what Amy was doing. When she reached his flank, he tried to nibble her jacket, as if he were trying to groom her in return.

"None of that!" Amy warned. The colt relaxed as she moved on to the body brush, followed by the mane comb.

"Wow, he looks terrific," Joni commented, looking over the door.

Amy stood back and looked at Spindleberry's golden bay coat that now had a soft sheen. "It's definitely an improvement," she agreed. "Will you help me groom the others and then get them ready for the trip? I want them looking as good as possible."

"Sure." Joni tried to smile, her face a reflection of what Amy was feeling. "Is there anything else we can do?"

"I checked my mom's books, and I found that the best remedies would be rose-hip tea and Maritime Pine. We're also going to have to find proper leg wraps," Amy said. "Ty will help Grandpa with the trailer."

Joni nodded sombrely and disappeared to start the grooming. Amy went to collect the herbal remedies. Her mother's neat handwriting had described how rose-hip tea added to their drinking water would keep the horses' kidneys functioning, and the Maritime Pine would give their immune systems a boost. The weather was a little cooler, but Amy knew the temperature in the trailer would be several degrees warmer than outside.

She went from stall to stall, giving the auction horses the remedies before slipping out to the trailer to add rose hip and Rescue Remedy to the drinking water she had stored in big plastic buckets. Grandpa and Ty were just finishing sloshing out the last of the disinfectant. As Amy crossed the yard, Jack began to coil up the hose, leaving Ty to sweep the foaming water down the ramp.

"What time are they supposed to get here?" Amy asked Ty.

"Early afternoon," he told her, wiping his forehead with his sleeve.

"Can I leave these with you?" Amy nodded at the two plastic containers of water.

"Sure."

"I'll be with Spindleberry," Amy added. She caught sight of Ty's frown as she left but didn't hang around to ask him what was wrong. She was too eager to get back to the yearling.

Amy was thrilled with the way Spindleberry was already responding to the small amount of training she had given him, and she had planned to spend some time teaching him to pick up his hooves before he left. "Hello, boy." She smiled as she let herself into his stall again. He shifted restlessly, his long legs making the straw crackle. *He's probably wondering why he hasn't been turned out with the others*, Amy thought as she tickled his chin.

She began running her hands down his legs. Spindleberry shifted again uneasily, but showed his trust in Amy by not stepping away. Amy looked for the leg that was carrying the least amount of weight so that the yearling would be as balanced as possible when she asked him to lift it. As she ran her hand down his left hind leg, Amy became aware that she was being watched. Straightening up, she met Ty's gaze over the door.

"Amy," he said, his eyes filled with concern. "What are you doing?"

"I just thought that if I could teach Spindleberry to lift his feet, then if someone was looking for a yearling to train, and he was well behaved when they looked him over, then…" Amy's voice trailed off. She knew it was senseless. There was no need to explain. She could tell by Ty's expression that he thought it was futile.

"Come inside for a while," he urged. "You've been working all morning. There's nothing you can do with him in the next hour that's going to make any difference at auction."

Amy's vision blurred, but she knew that Ty was speaking the truth. "Oh, Ty," she whispered. "I just don't know how I'm going to do this."

"For better or worse, there is nothing for us to do," Ty said. "They are going to come, and they are going to take the horses away."

Amy looked at Ty and knew he was right. What he had said sounded so cold, but it was honest. All their love, all their time, and all their remedies would mean little when the drivers arrived. All of their kindness would be forgotten when the horses reached the end of their journey.

No one felt like lunch, but they still gathered in the kitchen for cold drinks and fruit. The conversation was strained, and Amy felt torn between wanting to get the departure of the horses over and done with, and longing for every extra minute of time she could have with them. She glanced at the office door, which was still closed. "Is Lou coming out?"

"She's been in there all morning. She's probably buried herself in wedding plans," Jack told her, taking a gulp of coffee.

Amy felt a flash of irritation that her sister could even think about her wedding on a day like this, but she said nothing.

After another heavy pause, the silence was broken by Joni. "Duke's much better," she said. "He's walking in and out of the barn with no problems at all. Moving him into the brighter stall really worked."

"That's terrific." Amy smiled at Joni, not just at her news but also at her obvious attempt to make everyone feel better. *She's a real team player*, Amy thought, and was just about to tell everyone about Apollo's improvement when a horn sounded outside.

Amy felt her stomach flip over. "They're here."

There was a small white pick-up truck parked alongside the trailer. Two men climbed out. They were both dark-haired and looked to be in their forties. The taller of the two men asked, "Where are the horses?" He directed his question at Jack.

Before her grandfather could answer, Amy blurted out, "Do you understand how cruel it is to transport horses in that?" She jerked her head towards the trailer.

The men glanced at each other before the shorter one replied, "Look, we're just doing our job. We've been told to pick up five horses and the trailer, and we'd rather do it without any problems."

Amy opened her mouth again to argue and felt Ty's hand on her arm.

"I think you should know that there is an investigation pending against your company, and you may land yourselves in serious trouble if you knowingly drive those horses away in what would be inhumane transportation." Jack sounded very serious.

Amy glanced at the men, who both wore uncomfortable expressions, and then gave her grandfather an appreciative nod.

The shorter one spoke again. "Could you just show us where the horses are, please?"

"This way." Ty walked off in the direction of the barn with the two men. Amy exchanged an agonized look with Jack before following them. Ty led the men to the chestnut's stall first and unbolted the door.

Amy took one look at the gelding's trusting eyes and stepped forward. "I'll do it," she said.

The man looked as if he were going to refuse for a moment and then shrugged. "Suit yourself."

Amy felt like a traitor as she slid the halter over the chestnut's head. "Steady now, boy," she whispered. Tears blurred her vision and she blinked hard.

"I'll get the grey," Ty told her.

Amy nodded. She led the chestnut out of the stall and became aware of a second set of hooves clattering behind as Ty followed with the grey. Approaching the trailer, Amy's legs felt as heavy as weights. Her heart was pounding, and she suddenly knew that she couldn't let the horses be taken away.

Amy halted the chestnut and turned to face the men. "No," she said, feeling as determined as she had ever felt in her whole life.

The taller man sighed and stepped forward. "Look," he said. "We don't need your help to do this. Why don't you go inside while we load them?" And with that, he took the lead rope out of Amy's hand and pulled the chestnut towards the ramp.

Amy exchanged a desperate look with Ty as the other man reached out and took the grey's lead rope out of his hand. By now, both of the horses were starting to breathe heavily. Their eyes flashed and their ears pressed back. Amy was certain they remembered their last journey in the trailer.

Amy felt dizzy with helplessness. Suddenly, the kitchen door banged and Lou came running out.

"Stop!" she yelled, as she waved a single piece of paper over her head.

Chapter Twelve

Lou clutched the paper as she rushed towards them.

The man leading the chestnut stopped at the foot of the ramp and slowly turned round. "Look, lady, we've got a long drive ahead of us. And we've got three more horses to load." His voice was tinged with exhaustion.

"Oh, no, you don't," Lou announced. "You're not taking them anywhere." She walked forward and wrested the lead rein out of the man's hand.

"Hold on! The legal owners of these horses sent us to claim their property. We know our rights." The man's impatience was building to annoyance.

Lou's eyes flashed. "I think if you look at this piece of paper you'll find that the legal owner of the horses is, in fact, Heartland," she announced.

Amy's heart leaped as Lou handed the paper over to the men. After a few seconds, they looked back up. "I guess that's fine, but I better call just to make sure." The taller one shrugged his shoulders.

Amy wondered what her sister was talking about. What was on that paper?

They all watched as the driver pulled out a cellphone and dialled. He turned his back as he spoke. With a quick nod, he closed the phone.

"Well, it sounds like you were right," he confirmed, looking at Lou. "If I could just have the keys to the trailer, we'll get out of your way."

As if in a daze, Jack stepped forward and handed over the keys.

"Have a nice day," the men murmured as one climbed into the trailer and the other into the pick-up. There was a great roar of noise as the two engines came to life and the horrendous trailer rattled slowly down the drive, followed by the pick-up.

Amy glanced at Ty, Jack and Joni's faces, and saw that they all seemed to be in the same state of shock as she was. After a moment, Lou said simply, "I bought them all this morning." Amy could hardly believe it. She felt her shock turn into amazement, and she gazed at her sister with gratitude.

Amy slipped her arms around the chestnut. "You're not going anywhere," she whispered. "You're staying here, with us!"

As Lou watched her sister, a tiny giggle escaped her lips.

"You'd better explain," Jack told his elder granddaughter. "I'm not sure my heart can take much more of this!"

"I spent the morning trying to reach the owners of the auction house and negotiate a sale with them. It wasn't easy – they didn't even want to speak to me the moment they heard I was from Heartland. Apparently, we have a bad reputation with them already! I had to mention things like 'bad publicity' and 'legal recourse' to convince them it would be a bad idea to turn down my offer. Since they're in enough danger of being closed down as it is, they decided to be open to negotiation." Lou grinned widely.

Amy felt a huge surge of pride as she looked at her sister. "I can't believe it. All that time you were in your study I thought you were doing stuff for the wedding. I mean, it's incredible, I just can't believe it…"

"I think what Amy's trying to say —" Ty reached out and squeezed her hand – "is thank you."

Everyone laughed and thanked Lou, but she just shook her head. "I was only doing my part. It wasn't just me. We saved them together." Lou smiled at everyone and gave the grey mare a gentle pat. "So, do you think our horses would like to be turned out in their new home?"

"He's lovely, Amy," said Lou, leaning over the door to look at Spindleberry while Amy got a halter.

Amy shook her head. "I still can't believe he's here to stay."

She held out her hand, and Spindleberry stretched to graze his rough tongue over it. After a moment, Amy turned to look at her sister. "So, aren't you going to tell me how you did it?" she said.

"Did what?" Lou replied, dropping her eyes.

"Come on, Lou!" said Amy. "You know exactly what I'm talking about. How did you manage to raise the money to buy five horses? This morning, Grandpa said you'd both gone through the books and the money wasn't there."

Lou didn't reply for a moment, and then she reached out and put her hand on Amy's arm. "Will you do me a favour?" she asked.

Amy frowned and nodded.

"Can you wait to find out until later? I'm going to invite Scott and Nancy over for dinner, and I'll let you know then."

"OK." Amy felt a little hurt that Lou couldn't confide in her now. She noticed the concern in Lou's eyes and forced a smile. "Absolutely nothing else matters other than the horses being safe," Amy told her, meaning it with all her heart. "And that's all thanks to you."

Lou's expression softened. "Not just me," she said. "And we've only rescued five. I hope that Brad will have luck with the legal battle, so the auction house will be closed down and never be able to transport horses in those conditions again."

Both sisters were quiet for a moment before Lou said brightly, "Anyway, do you have some ideas about what we're going to do with our rescued horses? I mean, I know we won't want to keep them all here for ever."

Amy nodded. "I think the first thing we should do is to give them all names," she decided. "As for the future, the grey and the chestnut can be rehomed as riding horses, as long as it's on the understanding that it would have to be light flat work. They'd be ideal first horses for an adult beginner, since they both have kind, patient temperaments." She took a deep breath. "As for the two older horses, I guess they can be advertised as companions. Isn't it wonderful to think of them living out their retirement, being able to graze all day long in a big, lush paddock?"

Lou raised her eyebrows at Spindleberry. "And what about this young fellow?"

"Well, let's take him down to the paddock, and I'll tell you my grand plan," Amy said, opening the stall door.

* * *

As they walked to the paddock, they could see Joni sitting on the top rail of the fence. She and Ty had turned out the other four horses while Amy had been getting Spindleberry. "I just can't take my eyes off them," Joni confessed. "They look like completely different horses."

"I know what you mean," Amy agreed, taking in the sight. "I've been trying so hard not to bond with them. It's wonderful to know that we can really get to know them now."

"Yes, we've all been noticing how little bonding you've done," said Lou, looking meaningfully at Spindleberry.

Amy grinned. She led the colt through the gate and slipped off his halter. The yearling gave a playful buck and cantered around the other horses a few times as if he wanted them to join in. They all ignored him, and after a few circuits, he settled down to graze.

Amy and Lou sat next to Joni on the fence and filled her in on their plans for the horses. Joni looked delighted. "I've never worked with a horse that was in poor condition before," she said. "I can't wait to see them looking healthy."

Amy nodded. She shared Joni's enthusiasm. "We can give the younger ones some gentle schooling before we rehome them," she said.

"Now are you going to tell me what your plans for Spindle are?" Lou interrupted.

Amy hesitated. "To tell you the truth, I'd really like to keep him for a while, Lou. Even before you bought the horses, I couldn't help but think how much I'd like to train him properly, using Heartland methods."

Lou looked thoughtful.

"He hasn't really been handled at all. Can you imagine how great that would be? Seeing what kind of horse he would turn into, being trained using all Mom's own techniques?" She held her breath and looked anxiously at Lou while she waited for her reply.

"It certainly makes sense," her sister said slowly. "I know how difficult it was letting Storm go – and Daybreak, too." She smiled, and Amy knew that she was going to agree. "I think it's a great idea, in fact," Lou said. "Think of what a one-hundred-per-cent Heartland-raised horse could do as an advertisement for the stable!"

"And more than that," Amy said, "we could both work with him, Lou. That's the way it was supposed to be with Storm, but we could really make it happen with Spindle."

Lou gave her sister a long look. "Do you mean that?" she questioned.

"Completely," Amy responded.

"Oh, I'd love it," Lou exclaimed, reaching out to hug Amy. "Whoa!" Lou laughed as she almost lost her balance. "And on that happy note, I'll find Grandpa and tell him we have another addition to the family." She slipped down from the fence. "Then I'd better get cracking with our celebratory dinner!"

A little while later, Ty came down to the paddock and joined Amy. She was still sitting on the rail, deep in thought, daydreaming about Spindleberry. She didn't hear him until he was right behind her.

"Hi." She smiled.

Ty climbed up beside her. "Nancy just arrived, and I've been thrown out of the kitchen. It's a madhouse in there. Nancy's brought a mammoth casserole, Lou's cooking up a stroganoff, and Jack has roped Joni into helping him concoct some kind of giant cobbler!"

Amy couldn't help laughing at the picture of her extended family entrenched in the kitchen. "Hey, do you think your parents might like to come over and join in the celebration? After all, it's thanks to your dad that the horses were rescued in the first place. It'd be really nice if he could share the evening with us."

"I'll give him a call," Ty said, fishing his cellphone out of his jacket pocket.

Amy slipped down off the fence to give Ty some privacy and wandered across to the old black gelding, who was standing under the shade of a tree, gently swishing his tail. "You're here to stay until we find you a wonderful retirement home," Amy murmured, gently stroking his nose.

Ty walked across the field, giving her the thumbs-up sign. "Dad said thank you for the invitation," he told her. "Mom can't come, but he'd love to."

"That's great," Amy said. She glanced at Ty and thought he looked relaxed and content. "How are things with you and your dad now?"

"You know, they're really good," Ty admitted as they walked back towards the gate. "Ever since I talked to him that day he brought the trailer in, it's seemed different – like we're really hearing each other for once. I mean," Ty explained, "we talked through what we'd say to his boss, and we made it work."

"That's such good news." Amy slipped her arm through his. "He hasn't brought up your trying to find a better-paying job again, has he?"

Ty shook his head. "No. And the fact is, you couldn't pay me to leave." They turned to look once again at the rescued horses grazing contentedly, and Amy smiled, Ty's words echoing in her heart.

The kitchen was crowded and noisy when Brad arrived, and Amy noticed the look of uncertainty cross his face as he stood in the doorway. "Hi," she called, patting the chair next to her. "Have a seat. We're about to start."

Brad smiled and came over to sit between her and Ty. He was wearing a freshly pressed shirt and clean jeans and looked genuinely happy to be there. "I'm glad to hear it's all turned out so well," he told Amy.

"It's terrific news," Amy agreed.

"Ty's mom sends her apologies that she couldn't make it. She's working a late shift at the nursing home. But she asked if she could come over sometime soon and meet the horses."

"Of course. We'd love her to," Amy said warmly, passing him a bowl of stroganoff.

"How are the horses doing?" Brad asked, taking the bowl.

"They're doing well," she said warmly. "All thanks to you."

Brad looked taken aback. "Not at all." He glanced across at Ty. "It was because you all knew exactly what to do with the horses. I would just have put some food and water into the trailer and kept going."

"Well, Ty and I have picked up a lot of experience over the years. And we did rely an awful lot on Scott's expertise," Amy reassured him.

"I'm afraid I wasn't much help to you," Brad said. "I just didn't understand..." His voice trailed off, and Amy suspected he was thinking about the palomino. "I guess I hadn't realized how difficult your work could be," Brad continued quietly.

"But the rewards make it all worthwhile." Amy smiled at him, feeling a rush of joy. It was the first time Brad had ever recognized the importance of Ty's job.

"You must have been relieved when your boss gave you his full support," Lou remarked, joining the conversation.

"He didn't at first, which was worrying." Brad gave a quick half smile. "But Ty stepped in and backed me up. He said that he had a signed statement from a witness who was a licensed veterinarian. That kind of knocked the wind out of my boss's sails, and the evidence did the rest." Brad couldn't keep the pride out of his voice. Amy wondered if the change was as obvious to Ty as it was to her. Ty looked at her and the warmth in his eyes told Amy that he was as pleased as she was.

Everyone put the conversation on hold and concentrated on eating until Nancy cleared her throat and directed a question across the table at Lou. "Would you like to come and look at designs for the tent decorations sometime next week? I've seen some beautiful artificial vines that you can wrap around the pillars – in festive autumn colours."

Lou chewed her bottom lip. "Um," she began awkwardly, then glanced at Scott, who nodded and placed his hand over hers. Lou stood up, and little by little the conversation around the table stopped.

"I … I guess you should all know that I cancelled the deposit for the wedding tent," she began, giving Scott a weak smile. "I used the money to pay for the auction horses." She looked apologetically at Amy. "I'm sorry I didn't tell you earlier, but I felt I needed to tell Scott first."

Amy felt so proud of her sister. She knew how difficult the decision must have been, and she was impressed that Lou made the safety of the horses her priority. Amy wondered if this meant that Lou and Scott would have to delay the wedding. With a pang of guilt, Amy couldn't help but think how nice it would be to have her sister around at Heartland for a little longer.

Jack voiced Amy's question. "What does that mean for your wedding plans?"

"It's still very much on," Lou reassured him. "It's just that we're going to have to go for a cheaper tent now. It'll be smaller, so we'll have fewer guests, but we don't mind. The most important thing is that our families will be sharing the day with us." She glanced awkwardly at Nancy, and Amy guessed she was hoping that Nancy wouldn't be hurt by her cancellation.

The older woman stood up and walked around the table to

envelop Lou in a warm hug. "You made the right choice," Nancy told her.

"I'm so sorry to have cancelled on your friend," Lou said, stepping back. "I hope he won't give you a hard time because I changed the reservation."

"Oh, Lou, he'll understand," Nancy promised. "And if he doesn't, I'll just bring him out to meet those beautiful horses that your money has saved! Then he'll get the idea."

"And what about you, Scott?" Jack asked. "Are you OK with this?"

Scott grinned. "I know what's good for me – and that's not to come between my fiancée and Heartland!"

Lou gave Scott a playful jab, but even she had to laugh.

"How about we come up with some names for the new Heartland residents?" Ty prompted when the laughter had died down.

Amy looked at Lou. "Well? You should have first choice, since they're technically yours!"

"I can't name them all!" Lou laughed. "Besides, I bought them for Heartland, so they're all of ours."

"How about we put everyone's name into a bowl, and the first four names pulled out get to choose a horse's name?" Jack suggested, going across to the bookshelf to rummage for some paper and pens.

"Not me, though," Amy said hurriedly. "I've already named Spindle."

She caught Ty's eye and blushed as he pretended to frown at her. Amy knew he had been concerned that naming

Spindleberry made her too invested in the colt, but those worries were now far in the past.

Once all of the pieces of paper had been thrown into a bowl, Amy began to draw out the names. "Lou," she said, unwrapping the first piece of paper. Joni was called out next, followed by Nancy, who looked thrilled. The final name pulled out of the bowl was Brad's.

"OK," Amy said. "Lou first."

"Well, I wouldn't mind a name with a wedding theme…"

"I hope it's not Tent," Grandpa joked.

Lou grinned. "No, I was thinking more along the lines of something to do with music. What about calling the black horse Aria?"

"Lovely," Amy said. "Now it's your turn, Nancy. How about you name the bay mare?"

"I've always loved the word 'Shalom'," Nancy said. "It's the Hebrew word for peace. Would that be OK?"

"It's beautiful," Lou said warmly.

"Can I name the chestnut?" Joni asked. "I'd like him to be called Bear, after my mother's old pony that taught me to ride."

Amy smiled in agreement before turning to Brad. "The only one left without a name is the grey mare."

Brad cleared his throat self-consciously. "I know what I'd like to name her, but I don't know if it's the type of name you give a horse." Amy raised her eyebrows.

"Well, Liberty," he said gruffly, as if he were trying not to be sentimental. But when Ty gave him a nod of approval, Brad could not suppress a contented smile.

"It's a perfect name," Amy murmured, glancing across the table at Lou and sharing a look of delight. Liberty was exactly what Ty's dad had helped give these precious horses – and it seemed that no one recognized that more than Brad himself.

After dinner, Amy slipped outside to see Spindleberry again. Every so often the words "He's staying at Heartland!" would come into her head, and her heart would fill with excitement and shining rays of hope.

She leaned on the fence and whistled softly. Spindleberry stopped grazing at once and lifted his head. To Amy's delight, he broke into an easy canter and came over to her.

"Good boy," she said, pulling a mint from her pocket. Spindleberry gently lipped it off her hand before snuffling for more.

"Sorry," Amy laughed, "but I don't want you getting spoiled." Spindleberry was happy to stay with her anyway, and Amy spent a while just sitting on the gate, smoothing the fur behind his ears, talking in a soft voice about the future they would share together.

Suddenly, the yearling threw up his head and peered over her shoulder. Amy followed his gaze and, to her surprise, saw Soraya walking towards her. Her stomach lurched as she remembered the last conversation she had shared with her best friend. Picking up on her tension, Spindleberry snorted and trotted back to the security of the other horses.

To Amy's dismay, she could make out the deep crease of a frown on Soraya's face as she drew nearer. She began shaking her head. "Just what do you think you're up to, acquiring another five horses without telling me anything about what's going on?"

Amy felt guilt flooding over her. Soraya was as much a part of Heartland as anyone, and she had been left out of all of the recent events. "I'm so sorry, Soraya. It's just that everything happened so fast," she began, before noticing there was a playful sparkle in Soraya's eyes. Amy stopped, suddenly unsure of herself.

"Ty called me this morning," Soraya explained. "I was glad he did because I was worried when you weren't in school. He said that you all were going through a tough time. So I get over here as soon as I can and find there's a celebration going on instead!"

Amy laughed and slipped down from the gate to give Soraya a hug. "I'm sorry," she said again. "I didn't mean to leave you out, I promise. I had wanted to talk with you about it, but it's been such a weird week," she said.

"Oh, for you, too?" Soraya laughed, but there was a twinge of self-consciousness in her voice. "It's OK," she went on. "I haven't exactly been easy to talk to lately."

Amy read the expression in Soraya's eyes and smiled. There was nothing else to be said. One disagreement would never be enough to shake their friendship. "So," she said in a serious tone. "Are things any better with Matt?"

Soraya grinned. "Definitely. He's up at the house, probably on his second helping of dessert by now." She paused and glanced down at her feet before looking her friend in the eyes. "It turns out you were right. Things were never bad with Matt. I just thought they were. Ashley hasn't been chasing Matt after all.

She's been after Matt's friend, Ed, and that's why she was going to the basketball game – to watch Ed play, not Matt."

"Nice of her to make her intentions known," Amy said dryly.

Soraya exchanged a telling glance with her before saying, "Now that Ed's finally got around to asking Ashley out, her calls to Matt have miraculously stopped!"

Soraya stepped forward and linked her arm through Amy's. "I'm sorry I gave you a hard time, and I forgive you for always being right."

"Soraya!" Amy cried, giving her a playful nudge. "It was just a misunderstanding," she asserted. "And I'm glad it's over."

The two friends walked arm in arm and turned their attention to the field where the five rescued horses stood in a close group in the dusk, tails swishing lazily. "Now," Soraya announced, "we've got a lot of catching up to do."

Amy focused on the long-legged yearling, who was gazing at them with his ears pricked forward. She thought of the roller coaster of emotions they had experienced during the past week and wondered how she could possibly begin to find the words to describe what they had been through. Amy smiled as the colt dropped his head and began to munch contentedly alongside the other horses. When events had been at their worst, she never would have imagined that something this good could have come out of it all.

"Before I tell you the whole story," she said, feeling her heart fill with pride, "let's start off with some good news. Soraya –" she looked at her friend – "I'd like to introduce you to Spindleberry."

Don't miss the

Heartland ™

Special Edition

Winter Memories

"Unbelievable," Amy muttered, throwing a pile of horse magazines into a box. "She *finally* decides to visit and now everything has to revolve around her. She's not even getting here until next week."

Amy knew she was being overly dramatic, but she didn't care. It wasn't fair. She had had plans with Soraya for weeks, but now she was stuck at home with a can of polish and a duster.

Her sister, Lou, lived in New York City. She had a prestigious banking job, and hardly ever came to Virginia to visit. The last time she had stayed at Heartland had been in the spring. Now, she had suddenly called to say she was coming for Christmas, and, just as suddenly, Amy had to cancel her Friday night plans.

Amy kept grumbling, even though no one was around to hear. "I bet Lou's at some fancy wine bar right now having a great time while I'm stuck here cleaning her room." Amy had finalized arrangements more than a week ago with her best friends, Matt and Soraya. They all agreed the best way to celebrate the start of the holidays was a late night of movies, followed by pizza and ice cream. Amy had begged her mom to let her go. She had promised to clean on Saturday. But no, her mom insisted that it had to be done that very night.

Granted, the only reason her mom had asked her to clear out the room was because it was full of Amy's stuff, but that fact didn't improve Amy's foul mood. To her, it made perfect sense that her belongings should spill over into Lou's room, which was empty most of the year. Amy scooped up an armful of toiletries from the dressing table and cursed under her breath as half the plastic containers slipped out of her hands on to the floor. A lid came off one of the bottles and a cloud of talcum powder puffed up into the air before settling in a white ashy layer over the blue carpet.

"Great!" Amy muttered, dropping the remaining toiletries into a box. She heard a sound outside, and walked to the window. She pressed her forehead against the cool glass. *I could have been in line for popcorn now,* she thought in frustration.

She watched Ty, Heartland's sixteen-year-old stable hand, appear from behind the stable block. He crossed the yard towards his car, the full moon accentuating his high cheekbones and strong jawline. Amy sighed and ran her finger down the pane. For one crazy moment, she thought of opening the window, shinning down the drainpipe, and catching a lift into town with Ty. But she abandoned the thought almost immediately. She'd never do anything to get Ty into trouble with her mom. He'd only say no, anyway. Although Ty was always nice to Amy, he had complete respect for Amy's mom, who had been his boss for the last eighteen months.

Ty got into his car without noticing Amy watching from the window. She heard the faint rev of the engine and the car backed away from the house before disappearing down the long drive, the rear lights quickly fading from sight.

As she watched him, Amy began to sense that she wasn't alone. She turned around and frowned. The room was still empty. Then a movement caught her eye. A pair of white riding breeches had been pushed through the partly open door. As she stared in surprise, they flapped up and down before the door was pushed further open.

"Truce?" called a voice. A pair of sparkling blue eyes appeared behind the jodhpurs. "Is it safe to come in?" Marion asked.

Amy shrugged and turned to look out the window again, but it was more to prevent her mom seeing her smile than because she was still mad. She didn't want Marion to think she was so quick to forgive such a grave injustice.

"I think my offer of truce has come just in time. It's like a war zone in here," Marion remarked, walking in and looking down at the powder-covered carpet. "A nicely scented war, though," she added, bending down and touching the spilled powder.

"Sorry," Amy muttered.

"No problem. I can vacuum it up later," Marion replied cheerfully. The mattress springs creaked as she sat down on the bed. "Are you thirsty?"

"Not really," Amy said, with another half-shrug.

"Well, I was thinking, if we took care of the rest of the room together, we'd have time to watch a video with a mug of hot chocolate. What do you say?"

Amy let her shoulders drop. It was impossible to keep up any pretence of being angry when her mom was obviously trying to make up for her missed evening out. She turned around again. "Throw in some marshmallows and it's a deal."

"Done!" Marion beamed and patted the quilt for Amy to join her. "I'm sorry you had to cancel your plans with Soraya tonight," she said, and Amy nodded, accepting her apology but not quite able to say that she didn't mind. "I was just so excited by Lou's call that I wanted to start getting ready for her as soon as possible."

Marion reached across to pick up a silver picture frame from the bedside table and ran her finger over the photo of Amy and Lou as small children, playing on a seesaw. "You must have been three when this was taken," she said. "Which would have made Lou about eleven." She turned the photo around and propped it on her lap to show Amy. Amy knew it as well as any of the photos in the house. It had been taken the summer before their father's riding accident, which had left him temporarily paralysed. That accident had been the catalyst that had eventually divided the family. Her father had been unable to cope with his injuries and what they meant to his show-jumping career. He abandoned the family soon after he was released from the hospital. Just a few months later, Marion had left England to live with Amy's grandpa in Virginia. But Lou had been determined to stay in boarding school in England, convinced that their father would come back and they could all be together again. Though Lou's hope for a reunited family was not realized, she still didn't make much effort to visit her mom and sister in Virginia. Sometimes, Amy found it hard to remember that she even had a sister.

She glanced up to see Marion watching her. "I bet Lou's really looking forward to spending time with you," her mom said, as if she could tell what Amy was thinking.

Amy half smiled. "I'm not so sure about that," she confessed.

"It's never too late to start building relationships," Marion told her. "It's a shame that Lou can't stay to see the New Year in with us. Not that I'm complaining," she added quickly. "She's really busy with her work in the city, and she has lots of friends there, so she'll probably enjoy celebrating with them."

Amy reached up and plucked a strand of hay that was clinging to her mom's blue sweater. Marion could always find an upbeat way of looking at things, but Amy could tell by the strained lines around her eyes and mouth how much she missed her older daughter.

"You know, we'll have a lot to share with Lou," Marion went on. "There's the new training ring, for a start."

"You're right." Amy realized that it was just this summer that one of the pastures had been ploughed and filled with sand so it was appropriate for schooling. To save on costs, they had all pitched in to paint the perimeter fence. The end result was pretty impressive. Heartland would never have top-level facilities like Green Briar, the showjumping yard on the other side of town, but even Amy thought that the new additions made the place look really professional.

Amy had felt such pride the first time Marion had taken Pegasus into the ring and sent the beautiful grey gelding cantering freely around the perimeter. Since then, she had lost count of how many horses had been worked there.

"We painted the front barn in the summer, too," she reminded her mom. Soraya and Matt had come over to help whitewash the stable doors as well as the farmhouse weatherboards, and Amy had been surprised by how much fun a painting party could be – though Marion had been less than impressed with the white footprints that had appeared on the kitchen floor.

"I think Lou will be amazed to see how much work we've done," Amy's mom agreed, putting the photograph back on the table. "Your sister has such an industrious nature. She has a real appreciation for hard work done well."

Privately, Amy doubted whether Lou would be that excited about all the improvements, but her mom's enthusiasm was contagious, and she began to feel her own mood change. It didn't matter that her older sister had been away so long; she was going to visit now – and for Christmas.

"You'll have to show her how well Sundance is doing," Marion added, getting off the bed to pick up a bottle of deodorant that had rolled under the dressing table. Amy felt her heart sink at the mention of Sundance, but her mom didn't notice as she took an empty cardboard box and began filling it with a pile of T-shirts. "He was still so sick when Lou was last here. I think he had his final bout with colic a couple of weeks after she left, didn't he?" Marion went on. "I bet she won't even recognize him now!"

Amy thought back to how neglected Sundance had been when they had first rescued him from the auction house. If her mom hadn't bought him, the pony might even have been sold for meat. He was gaunt, his coat loose and shaggy on his frail frame, but his spirit was fierce. His long battle with recurring colic had made him a picture of misery, but when his bouts of sickness had finally stopped, thanks to intensive care and supervised feeding at Heartland, his condition improved a hundred times over. Now he was a handsome part-quarterhorse with superb conformation. Marion had asked Amy to help get the gelding back into working shape, and they had been overwhelmed by how well he had responded right from the word go. He adored jumping as much as going on trail rides, and he tackled every fence with a spirit of determination and courage.

Despite his dazzling work in the schooling ring, Sundance had always been unpredictable. Amy remembered well that it had actually been his bad temper that had attracted her attention at the auction house. He had snapped and stamped at anyone who had come near him. No one had given him a second look. Still, Amy was drawn to him – she was certain there was more to the pony than a foul attitude.

Sundance's recent behaviour would suggest otherwise. Over the last few weeks, he had been exceptionally cranky, and it was Amy who had taken the brunt of his bad mood because she rode him most. She couldn't figure out why Sundance had started to act up. He had done so well for her at the end of the summer, but every time she tried to work him now, the buckskin gelding misbehaved. Just the day before, Sundance had pulled at the bit and then stopped short in front of fences. Amy knew Marion would be more than willing to help out, but she didn't want to add to her mom's workload. Not only did Marion have her normal, demanding healing duties, she was trying hard to get all the short-term equine visitors back home for Christmas. And now that Lou was visiting, Marion would be even busier striving to complete Heartland work before the holiday. Amy crossed her fingers in her sweatshirt pocket that Sundance's bad attitude was just a passing phase that she could tackle on her own.

"I think Lou will prefer seeing Pegasus to Sundance," she said out loud, realizing she hadn't responded to her mom's mention of the difficult pony. "I mean, at least she remembers him." Amy knew that Lou had lost interest in horses after their father's departure, but Pegasus had been Tim's favourite showjumper, more like a member of the family than just another horse at their parents' successful showjumping stable. It had taken Marion a long time to nurse Pegasus back to health after the accident that ended his career as well as Tim's, but he was now fully healed and able to enjoy the trails as much as the other Heartland residents.

"Maybe we can persuade her to take a ride with us. She should be able to find the time since she's staying a week." Marion hadn't seemed to notice Amy's hesitation regarding

Sundance. She picked up the box that was spilling over with T-shirts of every possible colour. "Can you open the door? I'll put these away while you finish up here. As soon as you're done, come down. I sent Dad out to rent a video, so who knows what he'll come back with. What do you bet he'll have *Gone With the Wind*? He seems to think it's the only movie I ever watch!"

Amy grinned as she slipped from the bed and opened the door for her mom. Whatever video her grandpa ended up getting, it would be great to spend some time together as a family, just the three of them. She quickly scooped up the remaining toiletries and clothes and dumped them in her own room before hurrying down the stairs.

Jack was just taking off his coat and scarf. On the coffee table in the living room were the two movies he'd selected from the video store. Amy bit back a grin as she picked up the top one and opened it. "*Gone With the Wind*," she announced as Marion walked in from the kitchen with a tray of mugs. "Good choice, Grandpa."

Marion shook her head and smiled as she put the tray down on the coffee table.

"It's your mom's favourite," Jack said, pushing the TV out from the corner of the room so they would be able to watch it comfortably from the sofa. He glanced up and saw the grin across Amy's face. "What did I say?"

"Dad! I must have seen that movie a hundred times!" Marion protested playfully.

"Well, they don't make them like they used to," Jack told

her. "Besides, you always fall asleep if you're watching anything else." He clicked on the set and settled down in the middle of the sofa. He then looked at the tray in front of him and raised his eyebrows. "Hot chocolate and cookies? You're spoiling us, Marion."

"I just thought it would be nice to celebrate the start of Amy's Christmas vacation," said Marion, sitting down next to him.

"What she really means is that it was a bribe to get me to hurry up with Lou's room." Amy gave her mom a warm yet knowing smile and opened up the case of the second film. "*National Velvet*."

"Now don't you start complaining about that one, too." Jack held up his hands. "I had to drive all the way into town to get those."

"Us? Complain? Never!" Marion patted Jack's knee.

"No, really, Grandpa, *National Velvet* is great." Amy pushed the tape into the VCR and joined them on the sofa. Despite her earlier frustration, she couldn't help but feel content now. The best thing about any holiday from school was that she could spend more time with her family, and this one was even more special, with Christmas only a week away. "Happy holidays," she said, picking up her mug to clink it against Marion's and Jack's.

"Happy holidays," they echoed.

"To a wonderful time ahead, with the whole family together," Marion added, her eyes sparkling. "Just three more days, and Lou will be here, too."

Yes, thought Amy. *Three more days.* She crossed her fingers under the cushion on her lap, hoping that Lou's visit would turn out to be everything her mom was hoping for.